BRAND OF MAGIC

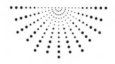

K M JACKWAYS

OLD SOULS PRESS

BRAND OF MAGIC

Redferne Witches, Book One

K M Jackways

Old Souls Press

ACKNOWLEDGMENTS

There is no way I could have got this book finished without the support of my family and my fellow Witchy Fiction writers. Thanks for the witchy discussions, reading the first draft, proof-reading and all the publishing support along the way.

ISBN 978 0 473 53758 6 (Kindle ebook)

ISBN 978 0 473 53756 2 (paperback)

CHAPTER ONE

*H*azel Redferne simply had to get to the pool. It was the only way to get rid of the voices in her head.

Not voices, she said to herself, wheeling her bike around the side of the house. *Feelings. Other people's feelings.* She gripped the handlebars tight and pushed off.

Her neighbour was leaning on his gate, looking amused. Joel was holding a shovel and his red-checked sleeves were rolled up to his elbows. Next to him was a freshly dug-in sign. He had seen her looking, so she should probably be polite.

"Are you selling up, Joel?" she called, putting her foot down.

He wiped his face with the back of his hand and nodded. "But hopefully no one wants her."

'She' was a beautiful section sloping down towards the city, with the odd spike cabbage tree, mature fruit trees, and lush native bush. Hazel could see the roof of the tiny house he had built himself from the verandah of her cottage. On summer evenings with the chirp of the cicadas and a rich fruit scent in the air, she sometimes wondered what the view was like from his place.

"That's such a shame," Hazel said. "Because it's a lovely property. What I can see of it from my place, I mean."

Idiot. Stop talking, she thought. It sounded as if she was out peering over the fence on a daily basis.

Joel shrugged. "Come and have a look if you want. I couldn't sleep this morning, so I thought I'd get the sign done."

He stood up and dug the spade into the ground with a stamp of his work boot. Then he leaned over and unlatched the gate.

"Alright." Hazel did have an odd curiosity to see what the property was like. From the front, huge bushes covered all but the tiny space where the gate was. She wondered if it was as beautiful inside as it appeared from her side of the fence. She dropped her bike at the front door of her cottage and took off her helmet.

Joel held the gate open for her. She sensed a certain melancholy from him as she passed by, and looked up into his face. He looked as if he had shaved with his eyes closed. He just smiled a little and gestured for her to go through. Joel's eyes were a really interesting shade. For some reason, she thought of the clear blue of Lake Benmore in the early morning.

On the right was an old garage covered in convolvulus and ivy, the wood warped from the weeds. Joel's tiny house was a two-story box facing down the hill towards the city. They rounded the side of the house and she saw an old armchair and a shiny wooden box, in a nest of sawdust. Up close, she saw that the timberwork along the verandah had beautiful detailing. She remembered that he used to be a joiner but she never saw him leaving the house in the mornings.

"What *do* you do for a job?" Hazel asked. He frowned and a lock of brown hair fell over his forehead. Rubbing the stubble beneath his lower lip, he looked at her like she was a puzzle.

"I mean, it's fine if you don't," she said. "Work."

Oh, Goddess. People often said she was a strange mixture of sensitive and direct. It probably stemmed from seeing the disconnect between people's thoughts and what they said. In her late teens, she despaired of ever being able to trust anyone. It had thrown her into a dark place for a few years. But the pain of those feelings, and her psychic ability, had faded a little as she grew older. Still, it seemed like it was a question he didn't want to answer.

He sighed, but it seemed like he was smothering a smile. "I have a wee business selling wood things, just at the markets."

He indicated the box, and she realised it was a linen chest. She ran her fingers over the smooth wood, admiring the trefoil carved into the sides in exquisite detail.

"It's pretty easy with a scroll saw," Joel said. "Come on, I'll show you the rest."

He walked down the hill and disappeared behind a row of lemonwood trees. Hazel trotted to catch up, pulling her jacket around her. She pushed through the overgrown bushes and emerged into a fruit tree grove, the leaves golden and russet. She picked her way around the piles of rotting feijoas and apples, with their sweet smell.

Joel hadn't stopped, and she followed him down to the end of the orchard. The property must be twice the size of her garden. To their left, an old-fashioned well was nestled into the corner next to the fence. She could see a few late

3

white flowers of the old kānuka tree in her own garden over the top.

An old dinghy sat beneath a weeping kowhai tree, its white oars resting on the grass. Hazel ran her hand along the side of the boat, where the name, Explorer, was written in cracked, peeling paint. Inside, green cushions invited her to rest. She caught her breath. Through a gap in the trees, past the city, the sun glinted off the harbour.

Now Joel was smiling and watching her to see her reaction.

"Is this where you bring all the girls?" she asked. His face fell and she realised that was the wrong thing to say.

Just then, they heard someone calling from the street. Hazel sent a silent 'thank you' to whoever it was, for rescuing her right then. Joel was already halfway up the slope with his longer stride and she hurried to catch up.

A man, with dark hair sticking up in spikes, was waiting on the verandah.

"How are ya?" Joel called. "Long time, Hills."

"I was just driving past and saw the sign up." The man leaned against the verandah post. "Where are you off to?"

"Not sure. Hoping it doesn't sell, so I can have some time to get back on track, to be honest." Joel looked down at the ground and kicked the toe of his boot into the grass.

Hills nodded at her. "Who's this?"

"My neighbour," Joel said and turned to Hazel. "And this is my cousin, Scott Hills."

As Hazel reached for Scott's hand, a cool pain spread in the knuckles of her fingers, like a sudden flare of arthritis. But his hand was firm and warm and she shook it. She covertly rubbed her hand with her other one and the warmth melted the pain away.

She couldn't tell anything like good or evil. The world was

not so simple as *that* – but she knew the chill of dark secrets when she felt it.

Hazel tried probing further with her senses but was too out of practice. It was like pushing through mud, thick and sucking.

"Have you got half an hour to chat?" Scott asked, and Joel inclined his head at her as if to check if that was ok.

"I better go get ready for work," she said. "Thanks for showing me around." She pulled out her phone. *Shit! Fifteen minutes. Just time for coffee.*

The pool would have to wait.

She flicked on the jug's switch and waited, staring out the window. Her tiny verandah was weighed down by wisteria and miniature roses. The rusting white metal table was loaded with plant pots and driftwood. An orange cat slunk beneath one of the chairs and curled itself down in a sunny spot, blinking at her balefully.

Cats were always hanging around. She blamed it on her ex, Hadley Fleming. Hadley was a kitchen witch with a rat familiar. He was not fond of cats – and therefore attracted every cat in Otago to brush against his leg. The cats didn't even mind her old dog, Bonnie, slumped at the moment in a corner of the couch, no doubt ready with some sarcastic comment about how late she was going to be.

The jug boiled and she poured hot water into the plunger. The rich smell of her favourite roast curled up around her.

She wiped the remnants of moisture from the inside of her kitchen windows and dusted under her pot plants with a sigh. Brown stems curled down over the sides. They were still alive, barely.

A knocking came from directly above her. Her Grannie Em was always more active than usual at this time of day. Hazel remembered why she had not had a relationship recently. Working was a lot easier than explaining *all of that* to someone new.

"Come on, come on." She willed the coffee to percolate through the hot water, thinking of the beautiful garden next door. She wondered why she couldn't pick anything up from the man's mind – Scott Hills. Usually, she got emotions from people – stress, excitement, wistfulness.

It would be like hearing a song in the distance. The beats were audible – that was the overall feeling, but she couldn't make out the lyrics, the actual thoughts themselves.

But this time, nothing. She had not practised magic for almost three years. What had she been doing for all that time? Working? Avoiding the gardening?

She checked the time and saw a video call from her mum was coming through. There was no time now, so she hit the red button with a guilty twinge. She whacked the lid onto her reusable cup, grabbed her linen bag and set off down the hill to the council buildings where she worked.

At work, Hazel found herself at the coffee machine more often than she should. She couldn't concentrate on this briefing for the new branding. She sipped her coffee and let her mind wander from the blank screen in front of her. She thought of the garden next door. It was beautiful and made her feel bad about her own garden's mix of overgrown and under-watered plants.

"Hazel!" Her boss's boss, Christo Stevenson, was walking

towards her. He knew her name? Hazel wasn't sure she had ever said more than two words to him before.

He did the odd talk or training session, but she would have sworn he had never even noticed her before today. She froze, ready to give him all the reasons why they had used their budget this month. She opened her mouth.

"You did good work on that 'People of the Octagon' campaign," Christo said. "It was right on the money – telling personal stories of why people moved here. Good idea, that."

Hazel let her breath out. That was unexpected.

He pulled his phone out and frowned at it. "Look, are you very busy over the next few days? I've got some work I'd like you to do for me."

She had to completely redesign the website for the new branding over the next two weeks. But you didn't say no to Christo.

"Yeah, I can do that."

"Come and see me in my office tomorrow first thing," he said.

For the rest of the day, Hazel couldn't concentrate, wondering what the extra work would be. Her mind flitted from task to task, landing for just an instant before it was off again. So she gave up, spread papers all over her desk and surfed the internet.

But one thing niggled at her. What was Joel's business all about? She searched his name and 'wooden furniture' and looked for a website. The background was a maroon colour with white writing. She had to squint to read it. It didn't even have online shopping integrated. It was a disaster.

By the time she finished work that day, she had decided she would get Joel's online presence looking professional if it killed her. Although considering her current workload and the mess she had to work with, she thought it just might.

CHAPTER TWO

*H*azel biked to the pool after work. The clock ticked over and she plunged into the water's cool embrace. At least twice a week, Hazel did her 30 lengths of Moana Pool. It was a cleansing of sorts. With earplugs and a cap, she wasn't distracted by her hair or the thoughts that normally flooded her mind. She focused only on her stroke and her breath and the strength of her kick.

Left. Right. Left and head turn. Breathe.

That was when nobody else was in her lane. This morning, a silver cap was coming towards her fast. She moved right over next to the lane rope, her hand brushing the plastic.

Don't you know this is my time? she thought to the silver cap, pulling the water towards her with powerful strokes. At the other end, she turned to head back towards the dive blocks. That cute lifeguard was standing there. She allowed herself a lingering glance at his arms and then dove back down into the water. She wondered how many times a week he worked out. Perhaps he was one of those men at the gym who grunted at themselves in the mirror. Maybe every day was arm day.

Hazel forced herself to concentrate on the stroke and rhythm. She was just building up speed when something cracked against her head. She stood up, clutching her cap at the front. Her forehead had collided with something really hard. She took out one of her earplugs.

"Sorry," Hazel blurted, expecting the woman to say it was alright.

"Ouch," the woman said, frowning beneath the silver cap. She was rubbing the crown of her head. "Just be more careful next time." She projected real anger, more than normal for a little incident like this. And a certain triumph.

"Um, alright." She paddled a breaststroke to the deep end, her head clanging like a bell. That wasn't fair. She was sure she had stayed on her side. A hand appeared beside her face – a male hand. She looked up into the young face of the lifeguard. He helped her peel the cap off.

"Maybe no more swimming today. You've got a fair bump coming up," he said. He gripped her hand and pulled her up out of the pool. Hazel must have been hurt, because afterwards, though she tried to recall it, she couldn't even remember seeing the lifeguard's biceps flex.

"Maybe wait here twenty minutes or so." She wrapped herself in her towel and sat in the bleachers until she started shivering. That other woman was still swimming as if nothing had happened.

Hazel got changed quickly and jumped on her bike in the chilly evening air. As she passed people getting out of their cars on Arthur Street, their feelings floated to her. This woman was stressed, fumbling her keys. This old man was unbearably tired and lonely, and he checked the letterbox for any note from his family. Hazel managed to mute the tide of feelings but couldn't keep out her own worries.

The more she thought about it, the more cross she got. Swimming was her time to focus. Now she'd feel out-of-sorts for the rest of the day. She never strayed out of her side of the lane and she was certain she hadn't today.

And why had that woman flashed her eyes at Hazel as if... as if she had won something? Hazel didn't like to lose.

When she got back, Hazel let herself through the wooden gate.

"Joel?" She called out as she walked around the side of the house. A grey cat jumped off the armchair and walked away.

She knocked on the door. There were no windows at the front, so she put her ear up to the door. She couldn't hear anything or sense any thoughts inside.

She wasn't sure why but she tried the doorknob. It turned and the door opened inwards. The light was on in the tiny kitchen. Joel was nowhere to be seen. Her eye fell on the table where a dark red business card sat at a haphazard angle. She stepped in and picked it up. 'Scott Hills, Passé Asset Management.'

"Hello," a voice said from behind her.

Joel's frame filled up the doorway. Damn, he must have snuck up like a cat. And here she was, caught in his house. Heat rose to her cheeks. He stared at her through narrowed eyes, his arms crossed over his chest.

"I came over to help but you didn't answer the door," she trailed off, lamely.

"I was out," he said, still squinting at her. "Help with what?"

"Look, I know this looks really bad. But after we chatted this morning..." *I couldn't stop thinking about you and your work.* She took a deep breath and mentally slapped herself in the face.

"Well, it sounded to me like you really don't want to have to sell this place," she said. "Would that be right?"

He let out a long breath. After what seemed like a really long time, he bent his head under the door frame and stepped past the table.

"Hot drink?"

"Yes, that would be great." She sat on one of the benches by the table, fiddling with the card.

"Do you always just go into other people's houses?" He stood with his back to her, filling the jug.

"Only when they live next door."

"Herbal tea alright?" He asked. At her nod, he pulled out some surprisingly fancy teacups and saucers from a hidden cupboard. He dropped a tea bag into each and poured the hot water, sending delightful fragrant smells into the small room.

"Chamomile and ginger," Joel said, setting the cup in front of her. He shrugged his shoulders a few times as if to shake off a weight.

She wrapped her fingers around the cup. Those two flavours of tea were perfect for relaxation and a good sleep. He was full of surprises.

"So... I'm guessing you are having money problems?" There was no easy way to approach the topic.

"What gave you that idea?" he said and laughed bitterly. "I'll be just fine."

She took a sip and the soothing warmth slipped down her throat. He really didn't like talking about this.

"Next door is my aunt's place, but I am thinking about buying a house of my own," Hazel said.

She picked up one of the coasters on the table, admiring the way the warm wood caught the light. It was carved in the shape of a kākāpō, the native flightless parrot of New Zealand, complete with a chipped-out beak and eyes.

"The wooden things you make are so beautiful," Hazel said. "I can help you sell more by working on your online presence if you like."

"You mean like a website? Cheers for that, but I already have a site," Joel said. "I just made those for fun."

"I can improve it a little for you," she said again. "That *is* what I do for a job."

He waved a hand. "It's all good. My customers know they can find me at the market anyway."

Hazel gripped onto the delicate cup handle, and to her dismay, noticed the tea bubbling up from the bottom. Curls of steam spiralled off into the air. He was really quite frustrating and she wasn't keeping herself controlled. *If he didn't want her help, fine.*

She sipped the rest of her boiling hot tea in silence and excused herself to go and make dinner when she was finished.

Hazel lay in bed that night and buried her hand in the soft, thick fur around Bonnie's neck. The dog was a warm lump in the middle of the bed, snoring softly. But Hazel's head throbbed, no matter which way she lay.

Joel's resistance had annoyed her, and she felt like it was her fault. She wasn't even sure what bugged her so much. Was it the fact that he didn't want her help? Or was it that he didn't believe she could? *Stubborn fool*, she thought. It didn't help that she couldn't tell what he was thinking.

————

It was the next night by the time the pain dulled to an ache. Hazel smoothed the tablecloth down again, ignoring Bonnie's judgmental stare. It was her turn to host the book club. Roasted chickpeas vied for space with gluten-free cupcakes, vegan savouries and sushi on her kitchen table.

She had been making excuses for a long while but there were no more reasons to put it off. It was only three women, besides Hazel and her cousin, Fritha. What could possibly go wrong?

She turned to the dog. "Just make sure you act like a dog, please."

Bonnie blinked. *Whatever else would I act like?*

"What did you say?" Fritha called from in front of the television.

She would never have got all this food made without Fritha's help. Her cousin had been more than happy to pop over that afternoon and help out, as they had both experienced Hazel's hit and miss cooking. Fritha's magic when it came to food and potions was far stronger than hers. Her pastries were heavenly, while Hazel sometimes burnt a pre-cooked pie.

Bonnie's ears pricked towards the front door. But Hazel waited for the knock before she opened it.

"Hiya," said Jade, holding up a bottle of something pink. "I brought the wine as instructed." She bustled through the door, and another woman followed.

Hazel stood out of the way as they hung up their jackets

in the entrance. "This is my workmate Mandy. I told you she was coming along, didn't I?"

"Yeah, of course. Nice to meet you." Mandy was shorter than Hazel but probably a bit older, as her tightly curled chestnut hair showed a hint of silver. She adjusted her white blouse that was tucked in at the waist.

A white top? Didn't she eat or drink? If Hazel wore that, it would be decorated with food splatters by the end of the day.

"Hi," Mandy said. They walked into the lounge, where Fritha was lying on the couch.

"I can't believe I've never seen your wee house before. We've known each other for two years, haven't we, Hazel?" Jade stood with her hands on her hips in front of the horseshoe hanging on the wall.

Fritha leaned forward to rummage in her bag. "Who wants to try my rhubarb wine?"

She walked into the kitchen and brought out some wine glasses. Hazel smiled gratefully at her and took a seat on the couch.

"Who else is coming?" said Mandy.

"Just June," Hazel said. "She's always late."

A hesitant knock came down the hallway and Hazel jumped up and opened the door.

"Hey, June! You haven't been at work 'til now, have you?"

June shook her head. The older woman's short hair was a little messy and she looked tired behind her glasses. Hazel resolved to find out later what was wrong.

"June, Fritha, this is Mandy."

"Hello," Mandy said in a small voice, reaching for a piece of sushi.

"She's the new collections officer at my husband's work," Jade put in. "Just arrived from Cornwall a month ago."

"Stepped off the plane and she had me choosing the next

book," Mandy said. "And I hadn't even met you all. I did love that bookshop in town, Souls of Scrolls, though. All the little paths between the stacks! It's gorgeous."

A series of clanks came from overhead and Hazel froze. It sounded like *she was dancing*.

"I haven't heard of that one," Fritha said loudly to cover the noise. "Anyway, what did you all think of My Cousin Rachel? I thought it was wonderfully creepy."

"Brilliant. By the end, it seems like the whole world is out to get him," Mandy said.

Nobody seemed to notice the noises coming from the attic. Hazel had given her grannie a stern warning but Em's philosophy had always been that she was old and she did what she liked. Now that she was dead, that was doubly true. *At least she can't get down here*, Hazel thought. And immediately felt guilty.

June was quiet tonight. Hazel sipped her wine slowly, trying to probe June's mind for a clue. Her efforts only met with static. Hazel's magic seemed to have dried up, just like her poor pot plants. She only had the faintest sense of people these days, the odd strong emotion, and she missed feeling like a key part of a group. She hated not being able to provide whatever was needed to help. Obviously, reading minds was *not* like riding a bike.

Fritha rummaged in her bag and pulled out a tin covered in kittens, offering the others a miniature croissant covered in chocolate. As Jade bit into hers and little flakes of pastry fell onto her lap, she seemed to come alive.

"Oh wow," she said, eyeing Fritha. "However long did these take to make?"

"Oh, it's nothing."

Hazel smothered a giggle as she thought of Fritha

conjuring the baking. It would have taken her less than a minute.

"How is your family, June?" Hazel asked.

"My daughter is coming back to live with me. To be quite honest, I am not sure how I feel about that."

June finished off the croissant and wiped the chocolate off her lips. "She's almost twenty-five," she said to Mandy. "Ridiculous, really."

"Was it a relationship break-up?" Mandy asked her, draining the last drop from her glass.

"Kind of," June said.

They all looked at each other. Jade stared at her wine glass, swirling it around. Fritha began refilling people's glasses.

They all knew the story. June's ex-husband had kicked her daughter's boyfriend out of his flat. So the daughter had left too, in protest. And now her daughter was coming to live at home again, while June was just starting a new relationship.

"Families, hey," Mandy said.

"Yeah," said June.

Something clicked into place in her head and Hazel choked a little on her wine.

Of course there were other witches in Dunedin. But they were hidden and they mostly kept to themselves. They showed themselves at night, at coven meetings in the hills and the valleys along the rugged coast.

During the days, they searched for green spaces, walking through the leafy Town Belt or reading in the gardens. They shopped at tiny places crammed in next to second-hand clothes stores and pawn shops, nodding to each other in herbal dispensaries, bulk foods stores, art galleries, and book shops. Places like Souls of Scrolls.

The next morning, Hazel was outside Christo's office just before 8:30. He wasn't there yet and she could see through the glass that the office was dark. His PA, Karen, hadn't arrived yet either. It was quiet up here. She could probably get some work done in quiet like this.

Hazel rattled the door handle. Locked. She still had wet hair from her swim that morning and the cold snaked down the neck of her blouse. She hadn't told her own boss, Sia, about this private meeting. She wasn't sure how she felt about waiting around up here, so she walked back to her own desk.

June came over and asked if she wanted to go out for coffee later.

"Did you plan a wee holiday for you lovebirds?" she asked. June and her new partner had been looking forward to a break in Central Otago, and Hazel hoped June had a great time. She deserved it.

June showed her the link for a completely renovated house looking out over Lake Wanaka. She whistled.

"How many bedrooms?"

"Only four," June said. "But I feel like I should take my daughter along with me now since she's back home. She's not herself at the moment. What do you think?"

As Hazel pondered how to say this was a ridiculous idea, an email flashed up on her screen. *Free to meet in my office now?* It was Christo.

Hazel attempted to shield the screen with her body but June raised her eyebrows at her. Oh well, she would have to explain later.

When she got up there, another man in a suit was sitting in the chair opposite Christo. She took a seat outside and waited. Karen seemed to be busy at her desk and didn't want to chat, so Hazel busied herself thinking of puns about wood; 'This wood look great at your place' 'Wooden you love one of these?' Hmm, she really was scraping the barrel.

After about ten minutes, Christo came out straightening the sleeves of his grey suit.

"Sorry, Hazel. Something has come up. Perhaps we can chat about it over lunch? One o'clock Monday at The Brewhouse?"

"Sure." *Great, now she had the whole weekend to stew.*

Hazel shut the screen door behind her, and two cats stared, disappointed, at the glass. The brown one licked its paw and the fluffy ginger had the grumpiest look she had ever seen on a human or animal. She stepped over them, juggling the picnic blanket, her book, and a glass of elderflower cordial down the verandah steps to the garden.

Why don't you just let them in? They'll never leave you alone. Her grannie's voice floated down to her from the attic window. Only her family could hear her, but anyone could see her silvery form, forever in her long nightgown. Once, a plumber had a nasty fright when she popped through the roof above him. But it had been easily fixed by one of Fritha's potions.

"I'm allergic to cats," Hazel said, for what felt like the fiftieth time. "And they are strays."

You know they aren't, my dear.

"Bonnie is enough for me. How many pets did you used to have?"

Familiars. Em was brushing her long white hair with near-transparent fingers, leaning out the dormer window. Just

18

below her, the window box was full of flourishing herbs and other plants, their green tendrils creeping over the eaves. Hazel was a little jealous of her grannie's way with plants.

Well, at one time I had two rats, a cat, a monarch butterfly that I still think was spying on me – a lovely wee pūkeko bird – oh and a demonic chicken.

"How do you know if a chicken is demonic?" Hazel asked.

Fair point, said her grannie with a chuckle. *Now, I'm sure I heard an owl last night, which means a loved one is in danger. You should get to practising your skills again. And maybe talk to Briar. She used to finish my sentences for me, she was so tuned in.*

"I know." Hazel sighed. She put her book to one side. Eyes closed, she crossed her legs and pushed the garden sounds – a blackbird, a lawnmower grinding somewhere – out of her mind. She found that little dark spot in her mind's eye and teased it slowly apart.

Why did Christo want to talk to her in private? Into her mind crept the questions of why Sia didn't know anything about it and didn't seem to want to talk to her. It was unusual for her boss, who was normally so bubbly.

She heard a car leave in the quiet street.

Hazel looked up towards the window. "It's no use. I can't stop thinking about work. And it's bloody Saturday."

Joel's face appeared over the fence.

"Nice garden. Who are you talking to?" He looked around for someone else.

"Ah," she said, praying her grannie had hidden herself in time. "Just myself. Helps me work things out."

"What are you up to today, anyway?"

"Just reading out in the sun. Drinking in some Vitamin D." She remembered she was wearing her rattiest grey yoga pants. Did they even have a hole in the crotch? She stretched her legs out in front.

"Well, if you're free a bit later on..." He frowned down at the ground.

Hazel let the pause linger on a little, not sure what she wanted him to say next.

He cleared his throat. "I feel a bit shit, and maybe I am a little more attached to this place than I, ah... thought. I need to earn some money. Can't really go on like this."

She couldn't see his mouth, so she wasn't sure if he was half-joking or not.

"Can you – do you still want to help me out with my business stuff? Maybe tomorrow? You seemed like you wanted to help."

Humble pie. That was surprising. Hazel decided not to admit that she had been going to work on a new website for him anyway, whether he wanted it or not.

She smiled. "Whatever gave you that idea? Yes, tomorrow morning could work."

CHAPTER THREE

*A*s Hazel jangled the bells in the doorway, she noticed the plants on the living wall seem to lift, then sigh and droop down again. Teapots of red and yellow dotted with blue steamed on the counter. The café smelt of lavender and mint, and other herbs too, all combined into a smell that evoked her childhood home.

She'd taken her Grannie's advice and biked to her aunt's coffee shop in Roslyn. Briar was an empath witch too, and would definitely have some tips on how to work on her powers.

Briar was her aunt but the youngest of four sisters, while Hazel's mother was the oldest. Growing up, Hazel always went to her aunt with problems. Briar would wrap her up in a huge hug and give her all the answers. And if not, she would offer the exact flavour of cake that she needed and put on their favourite horror film. Now that Briar was the Secret Keeper of their coven, she was the one person Hazel could trust.

Sure enough, the cabinet was full of exquisite tiny cakes,

each topped with a colourful flower. A short woman in a headscarf and woollen poncho appeared behind the counter and Hazel smiled. Briar and her partner, Moira, were only ten years older than her but the generation gap sometimes felt huge.

"Moira! How are you? Is Auntie Briar here?"

The woman smiled, then immediately frowned. "You've got terrible timing, dear."

"Where is she?"

Moira stepped around the counter, holding her hands up. "Don't flip out. Bri is in the hospital. I'm going up there soon."

Fear gripped Hazel and she reached for Moira's hand as a reflex. As soon as she touched her, she sensed purple clouds of anxiety, a late-night phone call, hours of waiting rooms, confusion, frustration.

"What happened?"

"It was a sudden heart thing. She was found outside the toilets in the supermarket. Thursday evening, it was. I did ask Fritha to call you but she must have forgotten. We're all in a bit of shock. Especially her."

Thursday evening. So it must have been just after book club.

The words 'heart thing' sent chills raking up Hazel's spine. "Can I come with you?"

"Sorry, love. They don't want too many visitors at this stage but I promise I'll call you tomorrow and let you know how things are going. She is stable at the moment, dear, so that's one thing."

"Good." Hazel reached in to give Moira a firm hug, inhaling her scent of chai spice.

"The, ah, doctors seem pretty happy with her. They've done all the tests and can't find anything wrong. But one

22

more thing, I should tell you," Moira said, her eyes soft. "I sat with her all last evening, and this morning, I went back too. She hasn't spoken a word yet."

She hesitated. "You're both sensitive to thoughts. Briar might be able to communicate with you that way. Would you give that a go? It might give her some comfort."

Hazel sighed. For at least the last year, her sensitivity had been fading. She didn't hold out much hope of sending thoughts person to person either. *That* had never worked. She could communicate with her dog and her grannie, who was halfway between this realm and the next. That was usually quite enough.

And she was going next door tomorrow morning, so she wouldn't have much time to practise. But if she could give her aunt even a little reassurance...

"I'll try, Moira."

"Okay, so what is your unique selling point?" she asked Joel, doodling some logos on the pages of her notebook. "And let's think about what promise you make to your customers. Your brand style is home-made? Made by hand, made with care, made with love..."

Hazel rolled off some ideas, mentally shaking Joel by the scruff of the neck. He had no idea about any of this. All he seemed to be interested in was eating the muffins she had brought over. He stuffed what must be his fourth into his mouth. It was Sunday, and the autumn sun was shining brightly through the little window in the kitchen.

"Made by a tool?" He said and tried not to laugh, mostly because he couldn't around his mouthful of food.

She laughed. "Everything," she began. "Every little part of your business has to give the same message. Business cards, website, product tags. Every word of every little social media post has to tell the same story. And even the colours, fonts and pictures you use. What colours do you like?"

"Brown, I guess. Like tea. Want some?"

"I do, thanks." She stood up from the little table and stretched.

Joel had his sleeves rolled up again for the mild afternoon. He stirred the tea in one of those lovely cups that seemed to belong in a much larger house than this little wooden cabin. It smelt like strawberry tea this time.

"When you get all this stuff right, people will *find you*. We'll get some of your products sold, don't worry."

He looked at her with a start. "Sometimes it's like you can read my mind," he said.

She blushed. *You have no idea.*

They drank their tea in companionable silence, Hazel making notes about colours and the font in her notebook. She had thought it would be a lot more awkward doing this work with her neighbour. She had only spoken to him half a dozen times before – when her bin went missing for a night and randomly came back the next day, when they exchanged spare keys, when the wind knocked some branches down in the street.

He was just so down to earth. He wasn't trying to impress her or pretend to be something he wasn't. The truth was she still couldn't hear much of his thoughts, only tell something of the sadness he felt. And you didn't have to be a mind-reader to see that. You could tell from his slow expelling of breath in the quiet moments, the faraway look in his eyes, and the way he didn't meet hers.

Joel's phone buzzed on the table. He picked it up and looked at it, and the little line between his eyebrows became more pronounced.

He put the phone upside down and drummed his fingers a few times.

Hazel looked at him and raised her eyebrows.

"Sorry, I have to meet someone," he said.

"That's alright. I'll write up a few ideas and bring them over tomorrow. And we'll get a new website going too."

"Cool." He was distracted and already halfway to the door

Hazel gathered up her notebook and walked out while he held the door open for her.

"Bye," she said. She walked around the corner and out to the gate. It was cooler outside and almost dusk. She wondered if he was meeting his girlfriend.

That's none of your beeswax, she told herself.

She pushed open the door of her house. Bonnie trotted around the side of the house and came up the steps. She often wandered in the evenings.

It is though, Bonnie said, pushing her head into Hazel's hand and sniffing slightly to find out what exactly she had been doing. *Your business, I mean.*

"It's not." She patted the dog's silver head. She was not going to have this argument with this animal right now. She had definitely seen and heard women at Joel's place before. She had seen a few different cars – a blue Nissan, a red Toyota. And why not? All *she* was doing was helping a friend out with a problem in a professional way.

Anyway, you don't have to worry about any other women over there now. But I barked earlier. To get your attention.

"Oh, sorry, Bonnie. I didn't hear." She rubbed her face into the dog's neck, letting the soft fur tickle her skin.

25

It was that cousin of his hanging around out the front. Doesn't smell right.

"Scott?"

He's got something, alright. Bonnie wheezed a little at her own joke, her head bobbing up and down.

CHAPTER FOUR

*H*azel rode her bike to the hospital, her bag of knitting shoved in her basket. The clouds loomed low over the harbour. Cool drops fell on her hands as it started spitting when she was halfway down the hill. She wished she'd worn gloves.

As she rode through The Octagon, the white Oamaru stone of St Paul's Cathedral rose up on her left. The volume of hope and thankfulness hit her all at once as a focused chorus. It was nice, but it was like a whole choir appearing on your doorstep to sing a personalised happy birthday. At moments like this, she remembered how distracting it had been hearing every thought around her. That was part of the reason why she had stuffed this part of her life so neatly away and, it seemed, thrown away the key.

The other part of it was when Hadley left. Her grannie had always said witches shouldn't be with witches. It seemed to be true, for her at least.

Hadley, a kitchen witch, cooked the most amazing food. He loved natural places, like the rugged, barren hills of Otago, where he liked nothing better than to spend the afternoon orienteering. But they both liked to be in control of things and tended to take the easy way out instead of working at it. And one car didn't need two drivers. In fact, it made for a bumpy ride.

So, she had worked. When she first got her job at the Council, she had used her magic. Had used it earnestly to discover what her bosses and the customers wanted. But as she was promoted to Marketing Team Leader, people began to question if she was too spot-on. And so, she went back to basics, learning about audiences and strategy and searching online when she wasn't sure. And then she worked longer and harder and forgot what it was to be an empath.

By the time she got to the hospital, it was raining hard. Hazel chained up her bike and carried her helmet inside, looking up at the forbidding mass of concrete that was the hospital. It was stiflingly warm inside. She went to the reception and asked for Briar Redferne.

"There's no reason for her not to be talking—" The doctor broke off when she opened the door. She looked a little frustrated.

"Oh, hi," Fritha said. "It's okay, she's just my cousin. No *medical* reason."

The doctor pursed her lips, but she seemed sympathetic.

"Well, just keep talking to your mum." The doctor patted Fritha on the shoulder and left the room, closing the door behind her.

Moira was sitting in the corner and raised her thermos of tea in a silent hello.

Fritha sat in the windowsill, and Hazel went over to see her aunt. She was lying on the bed with her eyes open and looked perfectly fine. Her silver-blond hair was splayed out on the pillow. But she didn't move when Hazel crept over to the bed. She didn't focus her eyes, just kept staring out the window.

"Hi Briar," she said, feeling a little foolish. "How are you?"

Her aunt blinked but nothing else moved. Her face was a little pale, although her lips were full and pink.

"She is healing nicely, the doctors say," Moira said. "Fritha brought some of her wee concoctions along but nothing seems to have made much difference yet. I even burnt a candle this morning. That nurse wasn't too happy."

She chuckled and pointed through the window to the corridor at a fierce-looking nurse with her hair pulled back in a blond bun.

"We thought you might give it a go yourself," Moira said.

Hazel rubbed her hands together to warm them. Then she gently wrapped her fingers around her aunt's wrist. Briar's mind was devoid of any great emotion, just a little fear. Flashes of a clear blue sky appeared. Thoughts circled, like burger wrappers in a gust of wind.

Pansy. Pillow. Passé.

It was just random thoughts. She shook her head at the others but asked Fritha to put another pillow behind her mother's back, just in case that was what she needed.

Hazel worked on the scarf she was knitting, eyeing the rain sheeting down outside. She stayed for an hour. They were mostly happy to be silent, but now and then, Moira would tell them some little story about one of the customers in the cafe. Then Hazel asked Fritha if she could drop her home. Her bike would fit in the back and she felt her cousin needed some time-out from the hospital.

Joel was waiting for her on the steps when Fritha parked the car outside. It wasn't so much a driveway as a grass verge, marked with mud tracks in a wide curve.

Fritha looked at her with her brows raised and said, "Who's this? He is—"

"Just my neighbour," Hazel put in. He did look as if he had showered today, and he had on a brown t-shirt that made his arms look tanned. *His favourite colour*, she thought.

She opened the door and ran to the porch. "Hi," she said. "This is my friend, Fritha."

He stood up and ran his hand through his hair. "Sorry to wait here. Just keeping out of the rain. I kind of locked myself out when I went to the gym."

Fritha laughed.

"Ok, I'll get you the spare key," Hazel said. "Come in for a cuppa if you like." She unlocked the door and stepped over Bonnie, then followed Fritha into the kitchen.

"I've never been to *your place* before," Joel called from the hall.

Fritha whispered, "So, has *it* always been at his?" She twiddled her fingers and three cups zoomed down from the hooks and landed neatly in a row on the bench.

"Haha bloody ha," Hazel said, reaching up to unhook the key from its place behind the hanging bushels of bay leaves. They smelt fragrant and almost ready to use.

Pushing open the door, she saw Joel sitting in the armchair with Bonnie's head in his lap. He was rubbing behind her ears, just the way she liked it. Bonnie turned around and looked at her with a maddening look of smugness in her brown eyes.

"I didn't know you had a dog! I've never even heard it."

"Yup – this is my old Bonnie," she said, placing the key on the coffee table.

"Must be the quietest dog ever," he said, grinning. "Good doggy."

Oh good, he is a dog lover, Hazel thought, and a warm satisfaction settled over her.

Then Joel sighed. "I had a call from the new bank manager this morning. It changes every month. I've banked with Continent Bank for the last ten years and they treat me like a bloody number!" He was stroking Bonnie's head over and over, almost automatically. "They were ringing to let me know they had an offer on my house. Don't know if I'm ready for that."

"Oh…" Hazel felt like her words dried up. He had said he was working with his bank. The financial problems were obviously a little more advanced than he had let on if the offers were coming directly to them. That meant the bank had taken possession of the house, didn't it?

Fritha opened the door backwards, balancing the three mugs. "I hope you like my special coffees. I added a little extra something to get you all feeling good."

Hazel sensed a lot of hilarity coming from her cousin. She hoped she hadn't added anything silly. Surely, she wouldn't. They hadn't played with love spells since they were both teenagers. And *that* had never ended well.

"That's an amazing coffee!" Joel looked surprised. "And I normally drink tea."

"You should try her baking."

"Aw, thanks," Fritha said. "So, what are you two up to today?"

"I'm helping Joel out on a project. Work-related," Hazel added.

"That's really kind of you," Fritha said, that mischievous look on her face again. "You don't have to do that. At all."

"Where's the bathroom?" Joel asked. Hazel showed him and then came back into the lounge.

"You seem like more than neighbours," Fritha whispered. "Why have you been keeping him hidden?"

"I haven't!" Hazel sipped her coffee, avoiding Fritha's knowing gaze. It *was* delicious, a perfect mix of creamy and strong.

Joel called to her from the hallway. "What's happening here? Hazel?"

Hazel's heart dropped. Had he caught a glimpse of Grannie Em's ethereal form slipping through the ceiling? Excuses ran through her mind.

Joel was bent over in the hall by the cupboard. "There's a bit of a leak here."

"Oh, is that all?" she said, relieved.

He straightened up and frowned at her. "It could be quite bad. Is that your cylinder cupboard?"

"Yes. It's just one more thing with these old houses." She put an ice-cream container under it but, seeing as the cylinder was old, she knew it would likely have to be replaced. Her aunt was in the hospital and she didn't want to bother Fritha with any problems.

Hazel sighed. She needed to get herself a new place.

"I've called you a few times over the last few days." Her mother's voice reproached her. Hazel had finally called her parents back after everyone left.

"Yeah, I know. Sorry."

"Are you alright?"

"I've been busy." When Fritha left, Hazel got out her notebook and went through some of her ideas with Joel. He nodded along from his spot on the couch, Bonnie's head on his leg. He seemed happy to go with whatever she wanted, and Hazel didn't understand how he could have so little care for his own business. His own brand.

Her father's face loomed up in the corner of the screen, the blue and gold cap he always wore pulled low over his eyes.

"Hi, dad. But yes, I am alright," she said. "But Auntie—"

"Briar's in the hospital, I know. And it was good that you went to see her."

That was only this morning. How did she find out already? Witches!

"She is awake, mum. But she's not talking. And they want me to try and communicate with her. But I can't seem to do much at the moment."

"That'll be the stress. You always have been a bit like that."

Hazel pulled her fingernail out of her mouth where she had been nibbling it and hid it under the table.

"This time it's different. I'm kind of worried that my magic is completely gone."

Her mother frowned. "Well, I've never heard of that in the coven. Are you just exaggerating?" She placed the phone in front of her so that Hazel could only see the grey top of her head.

"You wouldn't hear of it, would you? No one is going to advertise that they are no longer magical!"

"Do you want us to come down there, Hazel?"

Hazel shook her head. No, she did not want her parents staying with her in the tiny cottage. It was already full of ghosts and dogs. Not to mention the cats...

"No, I'm fine. And I'm keeping Fritha occupied."

"Good."

"What's happening in Oamaru?"

Her mother told her about their house insurance which had gotten ridiculously expensive, Hazel's other aunt in Nelson who had opened a nursery, another cousin who was coming to study medicine in Dunedin. Then she asked again if Briar was on the mend.

"Briar will be ok, I'm sure of it. But I have to get through to her," she said.

"You'll do it," Hazel's dad piped up.

"Well, just take it right back to basics," her mother said. "You used to be quite powerful, Hazel, when you concentrated. No intrusions, no emotions. You'll get there."

CHAPTER FIVE

*H*azel stopped at the street art of the Haast Eagle
on the way to work. It was a little off the
roadside, in a car park. The painting was taller than her and
it seemed to come alive as she walked towards it. The art
depicted the giant extinct bird as a series of silver and black
metallic squiggles. She loved the piece and the way it showed
time and movement.

Stepping up close to the concrete blocks, she reached out
and touched their cool surface in an effort to channel the
artist. Art often used to give her the goosebumps as she
sensed the deep feelings the creator of the work felt. *Nope,
pretty close to nothing.* Hazel sighed and got on her bike and
went to work.

The noise at work seemed louder than ever. The printer,
the coffee machine, even the tapping of fingers on keys was
too much for her today. Hazel glanced at her day planner on
her desk and remembered with a sinking feeling that she was
supposed to meet Christo for lunch. Worried about spilling
something on herself all morning, she only took one potato-

topped savoury at the office morning tea shout. She almost screamed when she dropped it on her satin shirt.

June was in a foul mood and wouldn't chat. Sia was extremely busy, so much so that, when Hazel popped her head in to ask if she had got her email (that took Hazel two days to draft, with well-thought-out arguments, subtitles, and images), she only said, "I did."

Hazel sighed. She couldn't do much until her boss got back to her about the new draft marketing strategy, so she took out her notebook and planned out the look and feel of Joel's new website.

Before she knew it, it was almost one o'clock.

The Brewhouse was one of those large, open bars in the Octagon that put on a decent enough lunch for the office workers. If you like steak or fish and chips, that is.

Christo was already sitting outside with an immaculately-dressed woman. He stood up when she came over.

"Hazel, I wanted you to meet my business partner, Kirsten. I'll get us some menus."

Hazel smiled at Kirsten, but she was confused. Kirsten wore a blue turtleneck and had a severe blonde bob, which brushed her shoulders. She was sure this woman didn't work at the Council. She pretended to look in her handbag for something, meanwhile trying her hardest to reach into the woman's mind. All she sensed was a vague curiosity from her.

"Christo has really talked you up," the woman laughed.

Hazel grimaced. "Oh.

She never knew how to respond when people said that. *As they should!* didn't come off the right way. Maybe something more like, *He's always blowing smoke up people's a—*

"I work with him on a side business. Our interests align with the Council, if you like," Kirsten said.

Hazel was about to ask what business when Christo came

back with the menus and passed them around. She shrugged her shoulders, regretting wearing her jacket as it was a warm afternoon. But she had to cover the grease spot on her shirt.

"I hope we can get straight to it," Christo said, passing the menus back to the wait staff. "As you know, I am impressed with your dedication and the work of yours that I have seen. I would like you to do a couple of things for me, if you would. The first is to give a presentation to the National Tourism Board about all the great ways the Council is marketing the region."

Hazel was taken aback. "Yes, I can do that. I'm just wondering why you're asking me?"

"Christo has assured me you are the best employee to do it," Kirsten put in. "We need someone who 'gets' how the millennials, who may be coming here to work, think. We want to show them that we know what they like and what the best way is to reach them."

Someone young then, she thought. "When is it?"

"It's three weeks away. We really want to show them that we understand the national and international market. You can share how your campaign had such high engagement."

She nodded.

"And the other thing – we noticed that your last name is Redferne. Are you any relation to a... Briar Redferne?"

"Yes. She's my aunt."

The woman sucked in her breath. Christo glanced across at her and projected an air of smugness.

The waiter brought their food and everyone was quiet for a while.

Hazel picked at her warm lamb salad. The lettuce was that bitter mesclun that left a sour taste in her mouth. She was still not sure what was going on exactly but decided to be honest.

"She is not well at the moment, though," she said.

"Ah, I'm sorry about that," Christo said. "We might ask if you can arrange a coffee with her when she's feeling better."

"I can do that," Hazel said. Then Kirsten started talking about when she used to work as a trapper in the Catlins. She zoned out, rubbing her right temple beneath her fringe as the beginning of a headache ground through her forehead.

It was only after she got back to work that Hazel realized she hadn't asked what their business was or why they wanted to meet her aunt.

"Ooh." Hazel let out her breath. As soon as she walked up the little path with immaculate white roses on each side, she knew she wanted to buy this house. She had called Fritha to meet her after work because she trusted her opinion. If it also gave her something to take her mind off Auntie Briar, that would be a bonus.

It seemed to have worked because Fritha was smiling just as much as she was. The house was set off the road up some steps, so they couldn't see it until they emerged through an archway in the pittosporum bushes onto a little bridge

The wood had just had a repaint in crisp white and the door was a delightful shade of green. The real estate agent welcomed them with a smile.

"I think you'll love this place. It's really low maintenance and everything's been done." His name was Warren.

Yeah, yeah, she thought. But there wasn't a lot to dislike. The price was good. The kitchen was newish, with a window overlooking the city. Hazel gasped as she saw a book nook under the mezzanine floor, filled with shelves for all her books and low window seats for reading and naps in the sun.

Best of all, there was a clawfoot bath with a window onto a private courtyard.

"Follow me out here," the real estate agent was saying. "This is how you get to the sleepout."

They walked down some wooden steps and looked out on a huge vegetable patch and some dark green pines with their tops at eye level. Warren held the door open to the downstairs, and as she passed through, the hairs on her arms raised up.

The agent flicked on a bare bulb. Hazel stopped dead just inside the doorway as a chill tickled the back of her neck. She felt the fear of a family, huddled in the dark. But there was nothing there, just a few old mattresses leaned up against the wall.

"What's the matter?" Fritha hissed, as they came out into the bright garden. "You've gone all pale. Well, more pale than usual," she said.

"I felt something terrible in there," Hazel said. "Like a great... movement and lack of control. And the combined fear of a lot of people. It doesn't make a lot of sense."

Warren stood by the kitchen bench, shuffling his papers, and looked up with a smile when they came back in through the verandah door.

"What do you think?"

"Why are the owners selling?" Hazel asked. "Who are they?"

"Lovely couple with older children. They built this place – well, not themselves. It's only about 35 years old and they've really maintained it so well, haven't they?"

"What happened—" Hazel stopped as Fritha elbowed her.

"We liked it but we do have some more places to look at. Thank you so much for showing us around." Fritha smiled in her disarming way and Warren patted at his hair self-consciously.

"That's a shame because I really liked that place," Hazel said, almost dragging her cousin down the path.

"That book nook though! Could you live there but just never go downstairs?" Fritha asked hopefully, but she knew that wasn't the way it worked for Hazel. "Come on, I'll make you one of my special coffees."

They jumped into Fritha's electric car. Hazel rubbed her arms, which were still cold. She could never live in that house. The very earth felt as if it didn't belong there. And she wanted to find out why. She searched on her phone for the address and 'history'.

Of course. The Abbotsford slip had happened there in 1979. 30 people were stranded on a piece of land. That could explain all the fear she had felt. Her head was starting to ache again.

She read it out to Fritha, explaining how chilling it had felt in that sleepout.

"That's horrifying - I mean, that you can feel what they felt all those years ago." Fritha looked genuinely sympathetic.

"Yeah, I guess it must be just such a concentration of energy at that one site."

"You will eventually find a wonderful place where nothing bad has ever happened," Fritha said. "You have to!"

Hazel sighed. It wasn't easy, that's for sure.

CHAPTER SIX

*T*oday, the tapping from June's desk seemed to be hammering inside Hazel's head. She slumped down further as she read through an email from Christo. It outlined where, what, and how long her presentation had to be. She read through it with a sinking feeling. 45 minutes! The longest she had ever spoken for was about twenty minutes as part of a training session. She started drafting up some ideas but soon lapsed to staring out the window, thinking of a tiny wooden verandah with delicious detailing around the edges.

I hope it's not too late, she thought. Joel's house seemed like a part of him. He had built it, and it was so practical and to the point, just like him. She couldn't let it be taken away. He had mentioned the bank had an offer on it, but she hadn't even said anything to him after that. She had been too preoccupied with herself these last couple of days.

She looked over the basic free website she had designed with a critical eye. That would be somewhere for customers to buy the products. It had a little tale about who Joel was and what had driven him to make these things, alongside some beautiful pictures in high resolution. The next important thing was the stories they told about the products, the emotional impact that hit the customers in the gut, driving traffic to the site.

Hazel emailed Sia telling her she needed the rest of the day off for a migraine. She only had a little twinge when she pressed send. She was sure it would be fine as she had worked a few extra hours here and there in the last fortnight. And Hazel never took the afternoon off. Sia would hardly notice.

She biked home at lunchtime and threw her bike down on the porch. Unlatching the gate, she ran around the side of Joel's house. He was sitting on the porch, and heavy metal blasted from his phone. He was sanding the side of a chopping board. He didn't look like he had showered in a while.

"I need a chest," she blurted out. "For my friend, I mean."

"Oh hi, Hazel." He raised his head to look at her, and she realised she was probably a bit sweaty from the bike up the hill. Why hadn't she stopped to do a little dry armpit charm before charging around here?

When he'd turned down the volume, she repeated, "I'd like to buy one of your chests. It's June's 50th this weekend."

Well, it was. The fact that she had only just remembered that now – well, that was beside the point.

He raised one eyebrow. "You don't have to buy my stuff out of sympathy."

"I'm not! Also, what's your email address? I need it to create social media accounts for you. I've set up your new website too. And then we can start creating social media campaigns—"

"It's too late for that."

"We can still…" Hazel trailed off, as she looked at Joel's face.

"The bank sent me a delightful letter saying that the offer is going to go unconditional in two days. No more working with me. That's that, I guess," he said.

He looked so sad that she wanted to go over and sit on his knee, wrap her arms around him, and pull him close.

"We can still—"

"It is too late." He went back to his work. "I'm busy right now…"

She listened to the rasping rhythm of the sanding for a minute.

"Just give me the chest. Here's your money." Hazel pulled out three notes and left them on the step. She stormed around the building and through the gate.

Bonnie lifted her head when the door slammed. *What have you done now?*

Hazel didn't answer, just sat on the chair and stared outside, and Bonnie ambled over and placed her head on Hazel's leg and looked up at her with big, brown eyes.

Hazel automatically patted her head and felt some of the anger drift away.

Why are you so keen to help him? He's not being a good boy. Bonnie nudged her head under Hazel's palm.

"I know." It wasn't that she fancied him, although his jawline in profile was quite nice. If he ever shaved, it would be, at least.

It was just that she didn't want to see his beautiful property sold to some people who wouldn't look after it. That would be such a shame. She didn't think she could bear to live here, while that happened next door.

He should be happy that you care about what is happening to him.

"Shall we go for a walk?"

She got the lead down and clipped it onto Bonnie's collar. Bonnie magicked it onto her neck. She didn't go walking much anymore but could manage a small block. Hazel hated to make Bonnie wear the collar, but people gave her funny looks if she didn't.

She walked through Mornington, up the hill past the shops. A few grey-haired people were smoking outside the pub. A young mother was pushing a pushchair, one hand holding a coffee.

Hazel was lost in her thoughts. She wanted to help Joel because it would be something she could do, something she could control. She wanted to feel like she was needed.

He must have had problems for a long while, Hazel. Bonnie said. *For it to get so bad with the bank.*

Something clicked into place. She stopped. "The bank!"

Perhaps she had been approaching this from entirely the wrong angle.

When she got home, a beautiful honey-coloured chest was waiting on her doorstep, tied up in a green ribbon. A tag displayed an email address. Hazel ran her hands over the wood, wishing she could keep it for herself.

She typed the email address into her phone and sent a message: 'Hi Joel, I know you think I am an interfering busybody. I promise I can help you. But you have to tell me *everything*.'

CHAPTER SEVEN

*H*azel felt sluggish in the water the next morning. She got to 12 lengths of the pool, and little stars wheeled around her vision as she stood up. She hoisted herself onto the side and sat with her legs dangling into the water.

"Are you alright?" It was that lifeguard. He tossed a kickboard and caught it, while he talked to her.

"Yeah, I think I'm getting a bit of a cold."

"You had a bit of an accident last week, didn't you? Hope it's not a concussion," he said.

"No, I doubt it would be," she said.

Hazel wondered what the lifeguard would say if she told him that it was more likely to be a gathering of malevolent energy and she needed to do a grounding. She smothered a laugh, imagining the blank look on his face.

"Have you seen that other woman again? The one that bumped into me?"

He shook his head. "Not that I'm aware of."

He walked off, twirling the kickboard, and tossed it to one of the other lifeguards.

Hazel left work a little early again that day. She walked out without looking at Sia's office and shrugged off the guilt she felt. Sometimes, a witch needed to do something for herself.

She biked through South Dunedin and along the beach. She stopped for a scoop of hot, salty chips in paper. She ate them with the wind whipping her hair around her face and the never-ending grey in the background. She drank a can of sweet, bubbling lemonade. She got back on her bike and headed past the bushes that she knew hid Forbury Park racecourse, and then it was time for the hills.

By the time she got to the walkway, the dark was gathering in and she was physically tired. Her thighs ached from the ride. But an energy was building inside her. It was *time*.

Hazel climbed down the steep hillside. Of course, there were easier ways and better times to do this. Some witches did it first thing when the light peeked over the horizon. Some did it in a forest or reserve, against a backdrop of birdsong.

But she had always had a connection with Tunnel Beach. Her training had been here, with her mother and the elder witches.

She stood on the promontory, and the wind was cool in her face. She kicked off her shoes and peeled her socks off, nestling her toes into the soil. She felt the solid rock and prickly sandy soil beneath her. She breathed in and out, imagining she was a tree with roots stretching deep into the land.

She cleared her mind of everything and looked for that little black spot. She teased it apart and probed the dam that had been set up inside her.

It stuck. She butted up against it. In her mind, she was water and she flowed around the walls, always pushing, seeping into the weak spots.

She reached out, in tiny tendrils, painstaking bit by bit, stretched out through the earth and up into the web of nature and things that grow and change. And she started to feel the vibrations again.

The stalks of grass beneath her feet quivered with life. Past lives and long-dead footsteps murmured beneath her.

She felt the many hours of work for a father to hand dig the tunnel, the joy of the family spending wonderful days at their own private beach. Then the terrible heartbreak of the family as one of the daughters drowned in the bay below. She was still down there, wandering the rocks of Tunnel Beach.

Hazel reached further and tickled the living things in the rock pools and the shallows. Snails, tiny flitting fish, and desperately clinging creatures inside their shells, all hovered at the edges of her consciousness.

She let herself feel. And she sensed the warmth and buzz of power gathering in her hands. The breeze notched up a level, lifting her hair from her shoulders and buffeting the sea.

She got home just after eight and dropped, exhausted, onto the couch. She should have a shower to heat her aching muscles, then she would massage her legs and feet with chamomile oils. Despite how tired she was, she also felt like a weight had lifted. For the first time in weeks, she couldn't feel the knots in the back of her neck.

You should have taken me with you, Bonnie said. *I can protect you, you know.*

"I don't need—"

I know.

An email flashed up on her phone.

'Hazel, I really am sorry. Come over now and I'll tell you whatever you want to know.'

She could imagine Joel's long fingers tapping on the table as he waited for her reply. It was that energy that seemed to thrum through him even when he seemed relaxed.

He was a bit of a hermit, tucked away in his beautiful garden and house facing away from the road. He could hide there, working on his business at home, and he seemed so happy with his own company. But he had this fire burning deep down that told her he wanted more.

Hazel was tempted to go over there but she knew she wasn't at her best. She stared at the screen for a moment, her mind blank.

'I'm going to bed early, but I'll talk to you in the morning,' she tapped out.

She flopped onto the bed and fell straight to sleep, Bonnie snoring at her feet.

CHAPTER EIGHT

*I*n the morning, Hazel showered and got dressed in her work clothes. She draped a long cardigan over the top and stepped into her slippers. After making herself a coffee, she walked over the dewy grass, letting the cup warm her fingers. It was still a little dark and the old garage cast shadows across the grass.

She knocked on the door and waited. It smelled as if had cut the grass recently. The door opened inwards and Joel stepped out from behind it.

"You're a bit earlier than I expected." He ran a hand through his hair but it didn't do much to help. He was wearing a blue t-shirt with a metal band name on it. His facial hair was growing a bit longer and patchy, and he looked dishevelled, but a smile split across his face when he saw her.

"Did I wake you up?" She stepped inside and sat down on the couch. As she sidled past, she still sensed that sadness but now there was something else too. He had a little spark of *something*.

"No. I was just making tea." *I'd love it if you woke me up.*

"Huh?" She looked at him. He was putting a green tea bag in one of those little teacups.

"I'm just making a cup of tea for myself." He lifted the cup. "I'm assuming you don't want one."

"Um, no." Hazel's face heated up. Either she was making up words that she wanted him to say or she had just heard his thoughts. If it was the second one, this was the first time she had sensed his thoughts since they met.

Perhaps it was the physical proximity that made her powers work. She had to find an excuse to get closer again.

When he sat down with his teacup, she sat next to him on the bench seat instead of opposite him as normal.

"Ok if I sit here while you tell me the whole thing? For support, I mean."

"Yeah, sure." *If you get any closer, I won't be able to concentrate.*

Hazel cleared her throat. Inside, she was singing.

"I'm not sure how you can help now, but... I guess I didn't want to tell you about it because I feel like a bit of a loser," he said.

"You're not! Things happen to *good* people."

"I guess." He leaned back and put his hands behind his head.

"I saw the website you made and it looks really professional so thank you for that. People who buy my chests and jewellery boxes – they seem to love them. I get a lot of people saying they are such a good deal. You can't buy one-off items like that anymore. And my stall is always popular at the market.

But about three or four months ago, I just stopped getting any sales online. And I really need those few that I was getting. I took a loan out and, well, the cashflow just didn't work. My bank was really good at first – they rang up and talked me through it. They offered to extend my credit card. Then I stopped dealing with it because I just couldn't face it."

I went to a dark place. He fiddled with one of the coasters, attempting to balance it on its side.

"I get it," Hazel said gently. She heard his despair but she tried to keep him talking. She needed to find out the whole story.

"So, then I borrowed a little money off a family member – thank God. That kept me going for a few weeks, buying new wood and tools. And I went to as many markets as I could, but with the colder weather, there were less people around."

"Then a couple of weeks back, I got a rates demand letter. It was just for a thousand dollars but then I got letters from the bank totalling up all of the unpaid interest. I really hate asking for help."

"Really? I would never have guessed." She smiled, and Joel laughed a little.

"I don't know, I guess money and me have never got on well," he said. "But this is not just me. It's absolute rubbish, the way I've been treated. I didn't know what to do. I – ripped the letters up."

Hazel was about to reach for his hand but he jumped up, pacing back and forth in the small cabin.

"I stupidly decided to put the house up for private sale. I thought I could sell it and move on and everything would be cleared. But this was my parents' section and it's the only thing I have left of them."

"I can't just let it go. And the bloody bank decided in the meantime that they would get on with a mortgagee sale, I guess."

"Oh, shit – I am sorry." She was quiet for a second, and the clock ticked over the seconds. The cabin was sparsely decorated and Hazel thought it could do with a few pot plants.

"Alright," she said. "Thanks for telling me all of that."

Hazel stood up and pulled her cardigan around her. "You need cash fast, right? Today, you tap into your existing customer base. You could email all your past customers and send them a 25% discount code and see how many sales you get," she said. "Show your bank that you mean to pay them."

He saluted sardonically.

"What I'm going to do now is go home and get some breakfast – Oh, I'm going to be late! I've got to get to work."

"Here." He passed her a banana from the fruit bowl.

"Thanks." She smiled at him.

"I can give you a ride too if you want." He pulled on his boots by the door.

"That would... actually be amazing," she said. It was 8.15 already. Work started in 15 minutes and she had a meeting with Christo at 9. She would never get there on time by bike. She didn't own a car for environmental reasons, but now wasn't the time to be overly principled.

She ran home and grabbed her bag, leaving the coffee cup on the bench. Joel had pulled his old car around to the front. It was mint green.

She jumped in and buckled up. The leather seats were cold, but it wasn't as cold as riding her bike.

"This is..."

"Isn't it lovely? It's a Zephyr," Joel said.

"I was going to say a gas guzzler and polluter."

He grinned, tapping on the steering wheel. "That too."

The radio was playing Black Magic Woman, and they were both silent going down the hill. Music often helped block the flow of thoughts, as the people around Hazel tended to focus on the melodies.

"Where shall I drop you off?" Joel said, when they were driving through the Octagon.

"Just anywhere here," she said. "Hey, how well do you know Scott Hills?"

"We played together all the time as kids," Joel said. "He gave me that loan I told you about. Gave me shit about it, but still, he didn't hesitate."

Hazel swallowed. "There will be something we can do."

I doubt it.

He insisted on double parking in the main street and dropping her off right outside the main entrance. When she said thanks, she distinctly heard his thoughts.

This pile is completely of my own making. You'll stay away if you know what's good for you.

She got to work at 8:33. Sia made a point of going to the coffee machine near Hazel's desk, just as she was unpacking her stuff from her bag. Sia nodded at her, mouth pressed in a line. Just to show her she knew she was late.

I see you there, Sia thought. *Young people don't know the meaning of hard work.*

Hazel looked at her sharply and Sia smiled. She definitely had not said anything. That meant she was hearing other people's thoughts. It wasn't just some weird connection between her and Joel. Of *course,* it wasn't.

Her powers were back. Hazel quickly got her notes ready and went into the meeting room. She couldn't wait to try them out.

Karen, arrived, looking stressed and putting her hair up in a ponytail. She worked for Christo. "He's on the phone, so he'll probably be a few minutes."

He always keeps me waiting, Karen thought.

June's voice cut through her focus. "Hazel! Are you alright? How come you were late today? That's usually me."

Hazel opened her eyes to see June sitting in front of her. Had she spoken or just thought it? Sia came in and found a seat at the other end of the table.

June raised her eyebrows at her.

"Minor emergency," Hazel said. "Nothing too bad."

You wouldn't know a real emergency if it hit you in the face, June thought. *Try being married to my arsehole ex.*

At least I was invited to this meeting at all. It was Sia this time. *How dare they pass me by for giving that talk – after all the hours I've put in here, all the people I've trained. They can ask my husband how much of my life I have given to this place.*

Hazel breathed deeply. This was getting too much. She rubbed her hands across her forehead as if to wipe away the thoughts.

But I keep waiting for him like a silly little—

Oh shit. That was Karen!

Hazel desperately tried to block the thoughts, and June looked at her strangely. Was her face red?

She had to get out of here – it was too much. All of the thoughts and people talking, all at once. She stood up but Christo came in and shut the door behind him.

"Let's get started," he said.

His mind was on his upcoming interview for an internal promotion, but he greeted everyone and thanked Hazel for helping out.

Hazel gripped her pen like a knife. It was one anchor in the waves of thoughts. "I'll take notes."

The meeting was one of the worst Hazel had had, and that was saying something. She'd had some terrible meetings. Aside from going on for almost three hours, this one was a traffic jam of thoughts and words. Hazel struggled to keep up with what people were saying, and when she asked Christo to repeat himself three times, he asked if she was feeling alright.

Christo went over Hazel's notes for the presentation, checking with the others for input. Sia went over her notes for the new strategy with a critical eye. June and Karen didn't say a lot but they *thought* plenty. She caught Christo staring at her a few times, and wondering if she was grateful, he had asked her to do the speech.

Hazel walked out of the meeting room and straight out into the fresh air. The main street of Dunedin was no better. She walked around the corner to a little cafe and ordered a double shot macchiato with extra cream.

While waiting, she pulled out her phone and searched for Joel's business on social media. She found one listing that had one good review and one terrible review. No wonder no-one was buying his stuff online.

Next, she looked for Jade's number. She crossed her fingers that her friend would be able to help.

"Jade, how are you? I am so sorry to put you in an awkward situation, but I know you work at the bank. Would you possibly be able to do me a little favour?"

It took a little cajoling and a promise of half a dozen of Fritha's croissants, but Jade agreed to look up Joel's file. *It is his house,* Hazel thought. *He's got the right to know who is buying it!*

Jade called back twenty minutes later when Hazel was walking through an alleyway.

"It's a little weird," she said. "Nothing was in the computer system against that address. I found the paper file on a colleague's desk. So I had a quick look during the lunch hour. The offer is in the name of 'Passé Developments Limited'.

Passé. A thrill of recognition passed through her and she knew where she had to go next. She couldn't wait to try.

"Ok, thanks," she said. "I'm eternally grateful!"

"But, Hazel – there was an email printed out on top that the offer had gone unconditional today," Jade said.

Hazel collapsed onto the bench nearby. It seemed as if every time she took a step forward, something pushed her back two.

CHAPTER NINE

*A*fter work, Hazel stopped in at the hospital. Moira was there, sitting in the corridor, looking as cheerful as ever.

"I brought you a coffee," Hazel said.

"Oh, thank you, darling," Moira said. The other one was for Fritha but it didn't look like she was there. *Oh well,* Hazel thought, *I'll drink it myself.*

She asked the question she had been dreading. "Has there been any change?"

Moira shook her head. "No, but they are talking about sending her home in a few days to recuperate with me and the help of a speech therapist." *As if that will do any bloody good. I have to look after the coffee shop.*

"Oh dear," Hazel said.

Moira stood up to go into the room. "Come on," she said.

"Actually, do you mind if I go in by myself?"

"Of course not, love." She looked closely at Hazel's face. "You look terrible. You've got big bags under your eyes - are you alright?"

"People keep asking me that," she said and laughed. "I think everything has got on top of me. How are you managing the café anyway?"

"I have my ways." She tapped the side of her nose. "Fritha's helping a bit, of course."

I feel terrible about asking her when she has study to do, but I don't have much choice.

Hazel slipped into the room and shut the door. It smelled of disinfectant and that ripe tang of food that was past its best. A tray of lunch, that looked barely picked over, sat on the table beside the bed.

"Hi, Auntie." Hazel went straight up to her aunt and grabbed her cool hand. Briar's face was turned toward the window, eyes open.

Her thoughts were much stronger this time. They hit Hazel like a jolt of electricity. This time the sky was a whirling vortex of threatening clouds. The wind whistled in the background and her aunt's voice yelled: *Passe. Pillow. Pansy. Passe...*

Hazel moved her lips and concentrated everything on sending thoughts, squeezing Briar's hand. *I'm here, Auntie. I'm listening.*

Her aunt immediately stopped screaming the thoughts. *Hazel, is that you? Help. Please.*

Hazel, I'm stuck. Each of her aunt's thoughts hit her with the weight of a swinging punching bag. *I'm stuck in here.*

It's going to be alright. What happened? Hazel desperately tried sending thoughts to her aunt, but she had no idea if she could hear them or not.

Hazel?

I'm here.

I... don't know what happened. I was holding a pansy. It flew out of my grasp. I fell. Then I ended up in here and I can't get out. I don't want to forget but I can feel it slipping away.

Her aunt's thoughts started rising in volume again as she began to panic. The wind noise picked up, buffeting Hazel so she could hardly think.

Please. Help.

You are safe. I'm here with you and Moira is here too. We will help you. A hot tear slipped down Hazel's cheek and dropped onto the sheet. Her aunt obviously felt her presence, whether she could understand the thoughts or not. So that was something.

Hold on, she thought. *Hold on.*

Moira was watching through the window as Hazel hugged her aunt's unmoving body. Hazel thought it must be awful being stuck inside herself. She quickly scrubbed at her eyes. Why was she being so childish when Moira was so brave?

She nodded to her and Moira came rushing in. "Are you alright? I thought you had eaten bad seafood! You didn't look good there."

Hazel smiled weakly. She didn't feel good either. Her head was spinning.

"Best place to be if you need a sick bucket, though," Moira said, tidying the things on the tray table into neat stacks.

"I'm just wondering... Where was Briar found the other night again? Was it a nursery?"

Moira made a face. "No, lovey, I told you – it was a supermarket. In South Dunedin. Why? Did you get through to her?"

"Do they have plants?" Hazel threw back the rest of her coffee, now lukewarm.

"They could do," Moira said. "We'd rather you told a few people about our café than brought flowers and things in here, though. Send your friends along there to buy their daily brew. That will help us out."

"No – not for that! Don't worry, I'll be back as soon as I can." She kissed Moira on the cheek and ran out.

CHAPTER TEN

*a*s soon as Hazel walked into the supermarket, she realised it was a mistake. Why didn't she just ring up? Streams of people walked past her, thinking about how lonely they were, who was waiting for them at home, what they had to do. The queue for the lottery was even worse. A young man in grubby overalls wondered what his boss would say if he quit on Monday because he had won. A woman fingered her handbag strap, debating whether she would tell her family if she had the ticket for 'the big one'.

The floristry section was just inside the door by the lottery counter, with pots of pink petunias and there! Next to the generic bouquets of roses were a few pots of pansies. Hazel pressed her hands up to her head and walked as fast as she could. She didn't care if she looked a little kooky.

To the right were the public toilets, so that must have been where Briar was found. She paused to sense for any recent violence but nothing came to her.

The office sign pointed upstairs, so Hazel took them two at a time. She pulled at the handle of the door at the top. It was locked with one of those coded padlocks. She slumped against the door, allowing herself a moment to breathe.

Then she ran back down to the Customer Services desk. She had to wait a minute for the woman to get off the phone, where she was telling someone they definitely hadn't made an order. The woman sighed and wandered over to where Hazel stood. Her name tag read Shirley.

"Hi, I was wondering if I could have a look at the security tapes, please," Hazel said.

"You'll need the office upstairs." Shirley's voice didn't change in pitch, as if she was asked this question every single day.

"I tried up there but it was closed," she said and smiled.

Shirley looked at her watch and nodded. "They would have just left for the day." *I should be so lucky.*

"Can you perhaps leave a message for them? Please?"

"Sure. I'll need the exact time and date and what was stolen. Was it your phone?" Shirley still sounded bored.

"No, my aunt was attacked. It was around 8:15 on—"

"No one's been attacked here. I would know." *I know everything that goes on around here. The stories I could tell!*

Perhaps gossip would get her interested, then.

Hazel leaned over the counter and whispered, "Someone attacked my aunt and she was picked up by the ambulance last Thursday night but whoever it was made it look like a heart attack. Please."

Shirley put her hand on her hip. "Oh! That poor woman in the toilet? Marge found her," she said. The bored look in her eyes changed to one of sympathy.

"Sure, we'll help you out, love. Write down your phone number here."

By the time Hazel got home, it was almost seven-thirty. Another long day. She threw her bike down on the front steps and unlocked the door. Her head was pounding. She was surprised to see Bonnie wasn't by the door or on the couch. It was cold inside.

"Bonnie," she called. She must be outside. Hazel walked through the house and noticed the kitchen light was on. A covered bowl was sitting on the table. Candles were lit around the room and scents of lavender and sage wafted through the house.

She lifted the cover off and the smell of chicken and corn made her mouth water. It had been a while since she had eaten proper food. She heated the soup in the microwave and sat down to eat, not even caring who had put it there or why.

Hazel got out her phone and searched for the company, Passe Developments. It was registered to an address in Invercargill. The Director was Kirsten Treleaven. *Okay, this was strange.* It didn't appear to mention her boss though. Hazel scrolled through the list of names and almost forgot what she was doing.

Her eyelids started to close of their own accord.

A tap came from the front door and Joel's voice drifted in. "Hazel? You home?"

"I'm out the back." She pushed her hair out of her face and wiped her mouth.

Joel stumped down the hall and stood in the doorway. He was wearing his work boots, jeans, and an old hoodie. Sawdust seemed to cling to him so that he always brought the scent of timber into a room.

"I saw your bike was there. I did knock a couple of times but you mustn't have heard." Joel looked around at the candles.

"Oh, sorry. I was eating dinner," she said.

"It's been a good day's work. I got three sales today." Joel smiled.

Hazel hardly had the energy to stand up. "That's really good."

Was that only this morning? It's been one long day, she thought.

"And I've been working on a new chest. I'm at the stage where I need the wood to show me what it wants. Sometimes, no matter how much you chip at it, you can't find its true beauty until you go with the grain. Sounds dumb, doesn't it?"

"Not at all."

"You look beat," he said, and his eyes searched her face.

Bonnie chose that moment to nose the porch door open and wander in with something hanging from her jaws.

"Ugh. Is that a rat?" Joel backed up a little.

Bonnie dropped it gently on the floor. It was not a rat. Hazel didn't know what it was but she could tell in an instant that it was nothing she had ever seen before. Its blood was dripping silver.

She ushered Joel out of the room and walked him out to the front door.

"We get some pretty weird rodents here," she said, pushing him out the door. She heard the thoughts swirling around in his mind. "And lizards."

He stumbled out onto the step, looking at her strangely. *She's lying. She wants to get rid of me.*

"Sorry, Joel. I'm so tired tonight," she said.

"I just came over to tell you that my lawyer got in touch. The settlement date is in two weeks. So, I'll be moving out then," he said and walked around the corner.

Hazel wandered back into the kitchen and sighed as she sat down. Bonnie looked up at her.

"I'm glad you didn't start talking in front of him," she scolded.

I wouldn't do that. She managed to look injured, lying down next to the 'thing' with her nose on her paws, sniffing gently at it.

"You still brought it in while he was here! Why would you do that?"

Bonnie let out a puff of air. Sometimes she was still more dog than familiar.

Hazel scooped up some of the soup. "Who did all of this?"

Fritha came over when you weren't here. I just told her that you needed some looking after.

"Oh, good dog," she said. "But you really shouldn't have brought that inside."

It doesn't smell normal and I thought you should see it.

"You didn't kill it?"

Of course not!

"So, what is it?"

I don't know. But I know who can find out.

Hazel got a paper bag out and Bonnie gently picked the creature up and placed it inside. Hazel started up the ladder to the attic. She pushed open the hatch, looking at her grannie's reassuring blessing keys hung around the walls. Starfish and spiky sea anemones decorated three walls of the attic. Collections of sea glass covered every surface. It was warm up there from the heat of the day. Em was sitting on the chair by the window, her white hair flowing long down her back.

Hello, love.

"Hi Grannie," she said. "It appears I've got my power back."

You haven't been up to talk to me in a while. I thought something must be going on. Well, apart from that nice neighbour hanging 'round.

Hazel sighed. There were no secrets here. "Today I could hear people from about a metre away. Even more."

Her grannie clapped her hands together. *That's so great—*

"No." She shook her head. "It's gone to the other extreme now. I can't think, I can't follow conversations. It's too much. My head aches like it's been hit with a sledgehammer. And I've got no energy. It's like when I first came into my power."

You just have to learn to control it again. You had those walls up all that time, protecting yourself. Now you'll have to go with the pain and use it as strength.

"What does that mean?"

You're a smart girl. You'll figure it out.

Hazel plopped the bag onto the floor and sat on the bed in the corner. Why did grandparents always say things like that?

A bird flew in my window last night, Em said. *So, expect an unwelcome visitor sometime soon.*

"Um, alright." Hazel wondered what would happen if she moved out of the house. Her aunt couldn't exactly rent it out with an overstaying spirit in the roof.

"Grannie," she started. "I did have something specific to ask you. I know your speciality was dealing with sea creatures." She flicked the plastic bag open, exposing the lizard-like thing. "But do you know what this is?"

Her grannie stood up, silently, and her long silvery nightgown trailed onto the floor.

Stupid, impractical thing. Hazel always thought she looked so elegant, but her grannie hated that every day she had to wear a nightie. *Such thin material, I don't know what I was thinking.*

She leaned forward and reached up as if to adjust her glasses, which of course weren't there.

Wherever did that come from? Have you been meddling in something?

"No. Bonnie found it."

Her grannie bent down to get closer but shook her head. *It looks like – no, it isn't that. This is some sort of magical creature, but nothing that I've ever seen before. I know exactly which book you need, though.*

Hazel climbed back down the ladder, wondering if she should go and see Joel. He would be a lot more upset than he pretended to be.

But she didn't really have the energy tonight. She wasn't sure what his black mood would do to her.

CHAPTER ELEVEN

*H*azel woke up to the smell of dog breath. Bonnie was standing over her, paws on her chest, wet nose inches away from her nose. Pushing her hair out of her face, Hazel looked over at her phone.

"Why didn't you wake me up earlier?"

Bonnie sniffed. *You looked like you needed it. You were thrashing around half the night. Woke me a few times.*

She felt black and blue all over too. She looked at her phone and saw a missed call from Jade, so she called her while waiting for the coffee to brew.

"Jade? How are you?"

"Good. I just called as I wanted to say something else about that file. But I'd rather say it in person if that is ok?"

"Yeah, sure," she said. "I'll meet you for a coffee at The Good Life. And do you mind if I bring someone else along?"

That could work nicely, she thought.

Work passed in a stream of other people's thoughts. Hazel kept her earphones in and her head down in front of her monitor. It made the thoughts a little more distant, but the stress still made it hard to concentrate. *At least it's Friday,* she thought. *Maybe I'll have to take leave next week.*

She walked along the back way to the café that afternoon to avoid people. She spotted Joel's car as he was slotting into a park and waited for him.

"Hi," he said and smiled. He really did have the nicest smile – it was sort of goofy.

"Hi," she said. "How are you feeling about everything that happened yesterday?"

"Oh, you know." He went a little quiet after that. And that didn't really tell her a lot at all.

There's nothing I can do about it now.

"My friend is meeting us at the café too. Jade, she's in my book club."

I thought this was a date.

Jade was already there, staring at her phone. "I already ordered mine on the app. I haven't got long. Work is really busy."

Joel went to order the drinks, and Hazel climbed into the booth next to Jade.

"So, I was kind of curious about that file. Remember it seemed a bit weird? I looked into it," Jade said, pouring herself some water. "It looks like the sale contract was accepted for an amount less than the valuation on the property. That's not allowed, for one. And there's a really short settlement period – you know, the time between the approval of finance and ..."

"... the possession date," Hazel finished. "Ok, well, the guy that came in with me – it's his house."

"Oh shit, Hazel. That's a real conflict of interest." She moved as if she was about to walk out.

"Jade, please." Hazel touched the other woman's arm, just lightly, and was immediately barraged with confused thoughts and guilt, but mostly anger. She gritted her teeth against it. "Is there any way we can get him out of the contract? He absolutely *can't* lose his place."

"The only way I've seen is for the purchaser to pull out because they couldn't get a mortgage. And there would be hefty penalties. He could always go through the courts. But you're putting me in the line of fire then." Jade looked over as her phone buzzed. "Oh, and do you know whose desk I found it on? Mandy – the one I brought along to the book club."

Joel came over with the coffees and two slices of cake. Hazel took a little of the mud cake on her fork and it rolled across her tongue – just what she needed.

"Thanks," she said.

"If your house is being sold, you should get legal advice," Jade said to Joel, examining her fingernails. She had brilliant red polish on them.

He looked a bit taken aback. "Yeah, I know," he said, moodily. "I think it's probably too late though."

"You're probably right," she said.

Jade drank her coffee and left soon after, saying she had to get back to work.

How dare you put me in that position? she thought as she sidled out of the booth. She had every right to be angry, Hazel supposed.

Hazel stuck her fork into what was left of the cake. She would see the book club girls this weekend at June's. That was going to be awkward.

Hazel blinked in the gloom of the bookshop, Souls of Scrolls. The shop was inside an old house and seemed to go on forever through tiny rooms, filled to the ceiling with spines of all colours. They covered most of the windows, and light slanted in through the gaps, making silvery rays of dust motes in the air.

This was one place in town where she could fully relax. The bookshop had been here since she was a child and Hazel loved visiting whenever she came to Dunedin. She had spent many afternoons in a corner filled with cushions, sharing books with Fritha. She weaved between the stacks and followed the corridor to the back of the house.

When Hazel found the room she was looking for, she ran her fingers across the textured covers, pulled out a particularly old and dirty tome and opened it up. Inside was a carved-out section of the pages. She pulled out the key.

"Hello," came a voice behind her. "Oh, it's you, Hazel."

Tui, the owner of the shop, stepped out from behind one of the bookshelves. "I like to check up when someone comes in here now. Especially this door. And I don't tell people where the key is now."

She plucked the key out of Hazel's hand and unlocked a door tucked behind a stack of books.

"My grannie – I mean, a relative told me you'd have this specific book. I'm looking for a book called The Aotearoa 'something'," Hazel said. "Apparently, it has a dark green cover with birds."

Tui put her hand on her hip. *Oh, heaven, help me. Another one after a green cover.*

This last room of the bookshop contained the oldest tomes. Most of these books were only available to borrow. The room was about the size of Hazel's house but extended up two stories. Huge ladders on wheels stretched from the ground to the top shelf.

"I know it has a blood-red spine, if that helps. And the pages are tipped with silver."

Tui looked at her, her eyebrows drawn together. "I actually think I know the one you mean."

She walked over to one of the ladders and pushed it across to the left, as far as it would go. It creaked to a halt and she jumped on and climbed to the top with surprising agility. She pulled a book out and almost abseiled back down. Tui looked about fifty, but Hazel knew you could never tell with witches.

"Here you go, love. Might take you a while to read."

The Aotearoa Menagerie was a huge book. "Perfect," Hazel said, holding it with both hands. The cover looked like it was covered in embroidered silk.

"I'll put it on your account if you like. Here, take the back way out. It's quicker."

Tui pointed to a dark tunnel, which looked much older than the rest of the building. "It's the second right."

She took the second right in the half-dark. Soon, she pushed a door and emerged into a concrete garage. The entrance was half hidden in the side wall. She walked out, blinking, into the sunlight of Moray Place.

Now, where could she hide the book while she went back to work? It wasn't exactly *subtle*.

Hazel's Saturday was spent relaxing in her back garden, reading about all of the creatures of the past, magical and non-magical. The book catalogued absolutely every species that a witch called Ahorangi had observed. She had travelled the length of the country, it seemed, and the names were in the Māori language as well as English and Latin. The book even described the sounds the birds made.

Hazel loved the feel of the old paper. She was taken right

back to that time when New Zealand was green with huge ferns and majestic trees; a rugged, dangerous landscape, alive with the calls of wildlife. So far, she hadn't found the lizard-like thing that had turned up dead at her place.

Shirley, from the supermarket, called her. She sounded excited. "Oh Hazel, good news for you."

"I got our security guard to have a wee search round and he found that footage for you," she said. "It's really really quick. I can't see any attack happen, even though I've watched a few times. But maybe you better have a look ..."

"Can you send it to my email?"

"We're not allowed to send them out really," Shirley said. "Oh well, I can maybe get him to send it to me then I'll forward it on if you like."

"Thank you so much, Shirley." She had made a lifelong friend in Shirley as long as Hazel kept providing her with juicy gossip.

That orange cat was picking its way along the fence, studiously ignoring Hazel. She went back to the book and eventually fell asleep in the shade of the kānuka tree.

Bonnie knocked into her leg with her snout, and Hazel woke, feeling groggy. Fritha was standing in front of her, and the garden was much cooler. She shivered.

"I knocked a few times," Fritha said. "Did you forget about the party?"

"Shit!" she said and sat up, leaning on her arms. "Look, Fritha, so much has happened. I don't know if I can go."

"Come inside and tell me about it." Fritha helped her up as if she was an old woman, arm under her armpit. Bonnie stayed next to her thigh as if stuck there as they walked up the steps.

She sat on her bed and Fritha sat at the other end, a sympathetic look on her face. Hazel smoothed the bedspread and told her cousin everything, even about Briar being stuck inside herself.

"And so, I think the next-door house thing – and your mum being in hospital – are related. But I don't know why it would be."

Fritha turned her phone over in her hands. "Oh, mum! That sounds awful," she said. "And poor you, being able to hear her and not help."

"Yeah, and I'm just exhausted with my powers coming back. I can't go anywhere near crowds or even a few people at a time. It is like constant white noise, or radio static, like I'm further from reality and hearing voices all talking at once. My powers have come back really strong, much worse than they used to be. Do you remember?"

"I was only a kid but I vaguely remember Mum talking to you about it."

Briar would be able to help. "I need to talk to your mum now," Hazel said.

"Me too," Fritha said. They both looked down at their hands for a minute. Then Fritha smiled, although tears streaked her cheeks.

"Come on, get up. We're going to a party."

CHAPTER TWELVE

"*I* feel ridiculous." Hazel held her end of the chest as they climbed up the stairs at June's place. Why did there have to be so many wooden steps?

"You look fine. Let's put it here," Fritha said.

At the top, she let her side of the chest down by the front door, and Fritha knocked. Hazel pulled the beanie hat lower over her ears. Hazel wasn't at all confident it would block some of the thoughts.

"It's worth a try," Fritha said. "Can't have you going all cuckoo on me."

June's daughter opened the door for them, pushing long, strawberry-blonde hair out of her face. She gestured to a table covered in presents. They put the chest gently on the floor.

"Hi," Fritha offered, as the girl didn't seem to want to talk. "Where's June?"

"Out here." The girl took out her headphones and opened a door at the end of the hall, then nipped in through another door to her room.

Hazel pulled a hip flask out of her jeans and took a sip of

the burning liquid. "It doesn't taste like whiskey, that's for sure," she whispered.

"Well, it was just about as expensive." Fritha had stopped to brew up a quick potion on the way that she said would muffle thoughts. Unfortunately, it contained both saffron and grated white truffle, along with a lot of other ingredients. Fritha had winced when she put in a generous sprinkling of both.

"What if I need to hear Mandy's thoughts?" Hazel had asked. "That would be useful, wouldn't it?"

"Each sip will only last 5 minutes or so. So if you time it right, you'll be able to."

They walked into the dining room. A few guests were inside, sitting on the couches, and some were out on the balcony. The dining table had a three-layer purple cake on it, with the number 50 and pink sparklers sticking out of it.

June was standing with a few women around her, laughing. A tall man in the group must be her new partner – Brandon? Sia, her boss, gave her a little wave. Mandy was nowhere to be seen.

June came over to say hi. "Youngsters! Welcome."

"Happy birthday! Look what we got for you," Hazel said. June opened the hall door and looked down.

"This? Oh wow, it's gorgeous!" She hugged Hazel and Fritha together. And all Hazel got was the smell of her vanilla perfume. *So far, so good.*

Jade came over and offered them a glass of bubbles. She was smiling perfectly politely, although it looked a little strained to Hazel.

"Hi," she said.

"No, I won't, thanks. I've got my own." Hazel held up the hip flask. "I've, um, been developing some allergies to wine lately."

"Okay," Jade said, looking at the flask strangely.

Fritha took a glass and lifted it up. "To June! You may not be the youngest but you are the youngest of us in spirit. You deserve all the best."

"What have I missed out on?" Mandy spoke loudly and tucked her arm through Jade's. Hazel thought she had already had a couple.

"Hi Mandy," Hazel said. "How are you?"

She reached down to her pocket as her phone buzzed. It was an email from Shirley.

"Sorry, all, I just need to check this. Is there somewhere quiet I can go?"

"Oh, yeah, of course." June showed her into her bedroom. She sat down on the bed and opened the email.

The video was distant and jerky. Hazel watched her aunt come into the supermarket, look at the plants, and then walk into the corner. *Oh, auntie.* She stood back, holding a plant in her hands. Then the next instant, the toilet door had opened and closed and Briar was nowhere to be seen. The plant was on the ground in a smudge of soil.

Hazel watched it again: her aunt came in, went to the bottom corner and picked up the plant. Then she disappeared and down came the plant.

This time Hazel watched it frame by frame. When her aunt picked up the pansy, the next frame had a flash of a person. She couldn't tell who it was, as the face was too blurry. The following frame showed a distinctive shape in the air right where the person hit her aunt. Her aunt went flying back through the door.

The shape remained, shimmering silver, for just an instant. A hanging crescent. A curse.

Hazel went out to take her leave. "Come on," she

whispered to Fritha. "I've found out how we can help your mum."

Fritha stood up quickly. "How?"

Mandy came over, her cheeks flushed. "What about you, Hazel? You'll have one of my biscuits?"

"Why not? I'd love to try one." She reached out to choose a cookie.

I owe you for banging into you at the pool.

Hazel almost choked on the biscuit and Fritha clapped her on the back.

"It was you," Hazel said. She realized the potion must have worn off.

"Oh dear," Mandy said, frowning, and led her over to the couch. "What's going on then? You can read minds?"

"Sometimes too well," Hazel said, wryly. "Why did you bump into me that day?"

"I can sense other witches. And when I came to the pool that day, I thought you were one. It's tough when you first arrive in a new place – hell, an entirely new country on the other side of the world. I haven't noticed many of us here at all, compared to London."

I'm so lonely here. I shouldn't have come.

"And I just wanted to be sure – I promise, I didn't mean to actually hit you, just get a little close."

Hazel popped the rest of the buttery biscuit into her mouth. Her mouth was still dry, but she swallowed with an effort. "But you seemed so angry after."

"Oh," Mandy chewed on her bottom lip. "I am pretty competitive, I guess. I could tell that you were powerful. But not quite as powerful as me. I know it's stupid."

That is a strange way to behave, Hazel thought. *And a bit mean. But not really malicious.*

"And then when I met you at the book club, you were so

78

lovely. I knew it was you because I got that feeling from you again. But now – you are more powerful than ever," she said, leaning in. "Did you know Fritha is one?"

Hazel sighed. "Yes, she's my cousin. Look, we are all pretty easy-going down here in Dunedin. I don't expect my friends to compete with me in much more than a game of Pictionary. But ..." She had just remembered something confusing.

"Why did you have that file on your desk?" Hazel asked, curling her fingers into the fabric of her dress.

Now Mandy looked entirely perplexed. "File?" *I've got no idea what you're on about.*

"It is a mortgagee sale of a property in Mornington. Patrick Street."

Mandy smoothed down her shirt dress over her knees, picking at a crumb. "That guy that has ignored all our letters?"

Hazel nodded. "Jade said it looked like it had been fast-tracked down the process. Why?"

Mandy's mouth fell open. *Oh God. Don't tell anyone.*

"That guy is a person," Hazel said. "He is a close friend of mine, and that property is on his family land."

"He still didn't pay us, though," Mandy said.

"But you could have treated him with some respect. Maybe worked with him a little."

Mandy stayed silent. Her face was drained of colour and she looked as if she was about to cry.

"Anyway, I suppose it's too late now," Hazel said. "I better go."

"Sorry," the man at the door of the ward said. He crossed his arms over his chest. "Only one visitor allowed in. And only close family,"

Fritha rolled her eyes. "Ok then, Gary," she said, reading his nametag. "Wait here, Hazel."

Fritha walked around behind him and pushed the button to open the door. As the glass was sliding back, she winked at Hazel.

"How has your shift been?" Hazel asked.

"Not too bad, you know," Gary said. *Better now that it's only three minutes until my break starts.*

Hazel walked into the corridor of the toilets and watched until Gary rang through to the ward and walked off down the corridor. She pressed the button and slipped through the door. A nurse was walking down the hallway towards her.

She must be covering Gary's break, Hazel thought. She walked past the nurse, her heart thumping. Hazel hoped she would think Gary had let her in before he left. She walked straight down the corridor without looking back, and let herself quietly into the room. Having confidence was one tenth of witchcraft.

The smell of burning sage hit her nose as soon as she opened the door.

"Oh, great. You made it." Fritha immediately held her hands out over the bed, palms face up. "I hope poor Gary is alright."

"Of course he is." Hazel placed her hands over Fritha's, and her cousin began to murmur under her breath.

Her aunt was lying on her back, eyes closed, and her chest rose and fell evenly. But when Fritha's lips started moving, Briar's breathing quickened and her body twitched.

No, no, I can't, her thoughts came to Hazel, faint and floating.

"Keep going," she whispered, and Hazel felt the energy flow through her. The point where their hands met grew warm. Fritha intoned the spell again, and power flowed like hot, sweet blood through her veins.

They both stepped back as Briar sat up with a start, her eyes wide with fear. Her hair stuck out from her head as if sizzling with static electricity.

Fritha lunged forward to hug her mum.

"Fritha," she said. "Hello."

A huge smile spread across her face and then her eyes closed. She fell back on the bed and Hazel heard the soft breaths of someone in a deep sleep.

The next morning, Hazel woke up feeling like she was hungover. She looked at the clock. It was after ten. Her mouth was dry and her head seemed to spin at the slightest movement. She couldn't stomach any breakfast.

Today was going to be a day at the beach all by herself – to ground and cleanse and breathe. She was supposed to be going to look at another house later on too.

She threw on a dress over her togs and then a jersey too. Dunedin in autumn could be sweltering or it could be like the depths of winter. All in the same day. She chucked her sunglasses on and packed a towel and book into her bag. She stared at it a moment with her hand on her hip and threw in her jacket too, just in case.

As she went down the steps, she saw Joel out on the street. She called out hi and he walked over to her. He wore shorts, and she didn't think she had seen his legs before.

"You look... like you're ready for summer," he said. His

eyes clung to her legs and she felt a hot flush rushing through her.

"So, do you," she said. "It's a beach day for me."

"Oh, that sounds great. Would it be weird – could I tag along?"

She shrugged. Time alone to ground would have to wait. "It's only me going."

"Well, I can drive us down then," he said, smiling. "You're sure you don't mind if I come?"

Hazel shook her head. "That means Bonnie can come too."

St Clair beach was pretty close to deserted, thanks to the chill wind that swept wisps of Hazel's hair up every now and then. She was glad of the jersey.

When the sun came out from behind the clouds, she pulled off her dress and walked into the water. The freezing water chilled her legs. When her body temperature adapted to it, she swam through the waves as she had done her whole life. The water soon blocked all the thoughts and the awareness of all the life around her. She could focus on herself.

Joel was sitting on the sand up by the dunes, staring out to sea. He watched her all the way as she walked back up the beach. She dried herself off and put her jersey on, then lay on her stomach on her towel and dug her fingers into the sand.

"So you swim at the pool a few times a week and come here on the weekend too? Aren't you freezing?" *You really aren't like anyone else I have met before.*

She nodded. "It's like, water energizes me or something. So have you got a place to go?"

"I'll find something," Joel said. "Crash at a mate's place maybe."

She frowned at him. "But don't you need to save up for a bond, get a moving truck sorted, all of that?"

He shrugged, fiddling with a piece of driftwood. Hazel couldn't believe he was still avoiding the topic.

She searched the dunes for Bonnie and saw nothing but a grey tail wagging behind a clump of bushes.

"Can I tell you something? I was waiting for you today," Joel said.

"How long for? I slept in this morning." She stretched out her arms. "It was amazing."

He turned to look at her. "Only about 10 minutes." *I couldn't stop thinking about you.*

"Joel, the truth is I don't even know you. We worked together on a project, yes," she said, but his intensity annoyed her. He was so hot and cold and she didn't have the head space to deal with it.

"But I don't know anything else about you – apart from that you owe people money." She felt a bit guilty saying that but she was still stung that he didn't seem to be giving anything of himself.

"That doesn't make me a bad person." He was quiet for a minute, and she listened to the hushing of the sea. "I'm nearly 30. I like listening to music really loud and doing martial arts. I've decided life is for living. I like eating Indian food, drinking tea, and I really want to visit Macchu Pichu one day."

"No, it doesn't make you a bad person," Hazel said softly. She looked down at the grains of sand, each one different, some sparkling in the sun, some dense and dark as night. She trickled sand slowly from her palm to join with the beach.

"What about your past? Tell me about it – it's not going to put me off."

"It's not relevant, though. I'm me. I am what you see here." *Take it or leave it.*

Hazel knew she could probe further if she liked. She was tempted, but it would be a violation.

Hadley, her ex, had been able to block his thoughts from her most of the time. Joel couldn't do that. There was a heck of a lot he didn't know about her either – the whole witchy thing, for example.

And he was troubled. She could tell that something had happened to make him sad, and she knew that she couldn't help him to be happy without knowing more about it. But if he couldn't tell her even basic facts about his life, how would he feel knowing she could reach in and take his most intimate thoughts at any time?

She sighed and put her head on her arms. She knew he felt like he was giving her something of himself. But really, they were too different.

"I don't have time for a relationship," she said. "I really don't. I'm sorry."

The waves crashed, endless and inevitable.

"You think you're trying to help everyone. I think you just want to control people," Joel said. "You didn't have to get involved in my work stuff."

Bonnie had appeared beside her, her wet legs dotted with sand.

Joel stared up at Hazel, defiant. Willing her to contradict him. His blue eyes seemed cold as ice today.

He looked like he wanted an argument but she couldn't think of one. Maybe she *was* just controlling.

Joel stood up. "Come on, I'll drop you home."

The car ride was quiet, punctuated only by Bonnie's panting from the back.

CHAPTER THIRTEEN

"*H*azel, I just wanted to reach out and connect with you ahead of our conference," Christo said. "Check that we're on the same page." He sat in the spare desk next to her and sipped an energy drink. It was Monday morning, and Hazel had already had two coffees.

"This is going to be such a great opportunity to align the business toward new synergies and show we are a leader in the space," he said.

Who talks like that? she thought.

"It's all under control," Hazel said and smiled. She had spent a few sleepless nights thinking about it. But now the speech was ready to present.

"I know it is. You always think of everything." He tapped the desk. "Great job on that strategy by the way. It was very forward-thinking. The Board loved it." *The Board loved me.*

"Oh," Hazel said. "My Marketing strategy for next year? I would have liked to present it to them myself, perhaps after the other presentation was done. It was my work." Hazel kept her voice even.

"Well, next time, hey? Anyway, have you thought any

more about arranging a meeting with your aunt? It would be much appreciated. But, you know, no biggie." He crushed his can and threw it in her bin.

He was still asking about that?

"Oh, I actually forgot about it. She only just got out of hospital." Her life had been ridiculously hectic recently. Hazel wondered why he was acting like it wasn't important but projected the feeling that it was very significant indeed.

"What shall I say it is about?" she asked.

"You can say it is a business proposition." Christo stood up. *I knew you'd be so happy I asked you to do this speech, you'd help me out with getting to talk to your aunt.*

"Sorry?"

"Oh, something has come up this afternoon. Can you make copies of this report for me?" He threw a stack of papers on her desk, with a thud.

As he turned his back, she wiggled her fingers. Just a little itching spell, aimed in the most awkward of spots, right between his shoulder blades. Hazel smiled.

After work, Hazel turned up Stafford Street on her bike. She glanced towards the mural of the eagle rising up at the side of the road, almost hidden behind the red building. She wondered if it would be any different, now that her powers were back. She kicked her bike stand out and walked up to the wall.

Hazel reached out to the cool uneven surface. Several things happened, almost at once, as her fingers scraped the concrete. She got a sudden sense of the artist, his anguish and sense of unjustness, his flow as he dipped into something bigger than himself and created the thing fully formed, his sense of pride, of leaving something in this country for others to see and marvel at. Her pulse was beating fast.

She sensed that she had claws and beneath her claws were cold concrete which bit and froze. She was cramped in an alien landscape, devoid of colour. But none of that was a problem because she could stretch to the left and out to the right, lift her huge metallic wings, and with one flap, she'd be up. Two huge powerful flaps and she'd be gone.

And she was hungry.

Hazel stepped away from the wall and dropped her hand, breathing heavily. That was intense.

Well, there was no time to think about that now. Perhaps her aunt would be able to explain it. Hazel had to go home and practise her speech to the sarcastic audience of one that was Bonnie.

CHAPTER FOURTEEN

*H*azel walked into the cold conference room half
an hour early. Her heart dropped. Aside from
being laid with carpet in shades thankfully not fashionable
since the 1970s, it had not been set up for the talk.

She scraped two tables across the floor to the front of the
room, then looked around guiltily and waved her hand. A
little art, some bright tablecloths, a sign by the door. She
gestured, and coffee and tea-making facilities and a jug of
water appeared on the long table near the door. The heater
buzzed open and started pumping out warm air. She wiggled
her fingers and chairs clacked open, one by one, arranging
themselves in rows.

By the time Christo and Sia walked in, with Christo's
business partner, Hazel was unfolding the last two chairs by
hand.

"Are you ok, Hazel? I should have sent someone to help
you with that." Sia stood against the wall and smoothed the
tablecloth next to her.

She nodded. If she hadn't used magic, she would likely be
seething mad right now. But as it was, she felt calm and

collected. She poured herself a glass of water and left it on her side table up the front.

She could sense that more people had arrived; the interest, the nerves, the polite boredom as they greeted each other with well-worked phrases. Fritha and June gave her an encouraging wave. She shuffled her notes and her hands shook a little. She hoped she would be able to block out all the thoughts.

When it got to five o'clock, she stepped up to the lectern. There were about forty people in the room. She was surprised to see Joel had just arrived and was standing awkwardly near Fritha.

"Thank you all for coming. I'm Hazel, and I'm one of—"

Drink it. She felt a thought coming from somewhere in the room. She swallowed.

"I'm one of the Marketing Team Leaders. I've been asked to speak to you all about the—"

Drink it. It was sinister and powerful and demanded attention. The hairs on the back of her neck all stood on end. She looked around the upturned faces.

Drink it. It was loud, louder than the other minds in the room. She tried to block it, reaching out into the sticky mud with her mind.

Christo stepped up to her and asked if she was okay. *I knew I should have done this myself,* he thought.

Get on with it.

"Sorry, just a second." She was about to reach for her drink when she noticed Joel lifting his hand about to take a sip from his cup of tea.

Pain coursed through her temples as she began feeling overwhelmed with all the thoughts. Her heart started beating an irregular thrum, and she put one hand to her chest.

She tried to force the thoughts back to a manageable

level. She fought, but the more she fought, the less control she had. It was like a current pulling her out to the open ocean. She was vaguely aware of voices and lights. But then she started to drift away.

Hazel remembered the cool of the ocean, her stroke, and the waves. She let the force of it batter her and then pushed back a little. Finally, she felt it give just a little. She sent her thoughts out in all directions, like ink on water, in one last blast.

She came to, blinking at the lights. Fritha was holding her head gently, and Joel was standing nearby. They both helped her sit up.

"Did you bang your head?" Joel asked.

"You just sort of swayed like a tree in the wind," Fritha said,

Hazel shook her head, and it took a second for the floating lights to disappear. Sia sat next to her in the front row of seats, looking at her worriedly. "It's alright. Christo will do the speech. Have you had an anxiety attack before?"

Christo stepped up to the lectern and started the presentation himself. It left a sour taste in her mouth to hear him speak her words.

When he'd finished and the applause was still going, she climbed up next to him.

He whispered, "Are you sure?" but he stepped down from the podium.

Hazel felt she had to do this. She wouldn't let a measly fainting spell stop her. She decided to go off script a little.

"The Council have promoted the region. The numbers are looking good. But it is really the people of our city that have done all the work. Working with the wonderful Sia and June, we have researched our audience by talking to them and spending time with them. They are the ones who matter.

Marketing isn't actually about sales. It's not about advertising. No, it's not. It is about sharing stories and love. But it is really about people, their hopes and dreams and deepest desires.

We understand the market so well because we know them. Because they are people. We are talking to our cousins, our aunts, that kid we went to school with. We encourage them to come here to Dunedin. We tell them that people here won't put up with any rubbish, but they will take you into their home and feed you. They'll take you curling and duck-hunting. They'll watch you try haggis for the first time.

We tell them real stories about what we all know, that Dunedin isn't perfect. But it is home."

After the talk, Hazel tidied things up at the front, while people left. Sia was trying hard to keep the smile off her face.

Even Christo had a comment. "That was an interesting perspective. We might have underestimated you. I'm sorry for it," he said, straightening his shirt.

While she was still gaping after him, Fritha touched her elbow and whispered, "It was pretty nice of your hot neighbour to come to your talk. I'll give you some space."

Joel was standing awkwardly to one side, wearing his checked shirt again and his work boots. He looked a little out of place among the suits and skirts in the room.

He smiled at her, one of those shy half-smiles that suddenly burst open. "That was brilliant. I'm glad I came."

"Thanks for coming along. Do you think I'll ever get a raise again?"

"You're lucky if you still have a job, aren't you?"

Hazel laughed. "You're probably right. I just felt like I had to say my piece."

"I wanted to come along and support you. And say I am sorry for the way I talked to you." He ran his hand through his hair.

"Shit, I'm always apologizing to you," Joel said. "I've been behaving like a bit of an idiot. I told myself that it's easier for you if I leave you alone. But I guess I'm a little more selfish than that."

"You can talk to me about it, though," Hazel said. "You're going through one of the toughest times in your life with the house being sold. Maybe... you could try not to take it out on me."

I'm coping again. Just.

"I'm learning," he said. "I don't think I have ever hung around someone who is just so on the same page as me. You seem to really get me. And being around you is just kind of easy."

Hazel fiddled with her bag strap. She felt a twinge of guilt.

"I am sorry too," she said. "I shouldn't put you under so much pressure."

She looked around. Only Fritha was left, standing in the foyer, with her phone out. Everything had been cleaned up. *Some might say unbelievably fast,* she thought.

"Do you want a ride up the hill?" Joel said. "Then we could grab some dinner?" Her stomach gurgled at the mention of food and she nodded gratefully

Fritha came over to hug Hazel goodbye. "That was so good. I'm glad you're ok."

"I feel fine now," she said. "What did it look like?"

"You just went kind of white and then flaked out," Joel said. "And at the same time, your cousin knocked my tea flying." There was a dark splodge on his chest.

"Sorry about that," said Fritha. She raised her eyebrows at Hazel to show that it was her fault.

She must have heard my thoughts, Hazel thought. *At the last minute.*

"I'll talk to you later," Fritha said. "Have fun, you two."

Joel opened the boot of the Zephyr, and she put her bike in.

He held her car door open, then leaned in until his face was very close to hers. "Can I?" *I couldn't wait.*

In response, she leaned forward for the kiss. His lips met hers, soft and insistent. He leaned back and smiled at her, before walking around to his side.

As he was driving, he put his arm awkwardly behind her. "So, my cousin rang last night. It turns out he is part of the company that bought my house."

"What?!"

"Yeah," Joel tapped the steering wheel. "I was pretty angry at first, but I suppose… it is what it is. Not much I can do."

Hazel was silent for a while, thinking about it. She knew that cousin of his had been planning something. And she hadn't said anything to Joel about it, because she was worried about giving up her secret. What if she had been able to stop the whole thing?

Joel's voice broke through her thoughts. "He said I can keep living here."

"That's good," she said. "Isn't it?"

"I think so." He shrugged. "Means I don't have to find a place. I can stay in my wee house."

"Do you know why he wanted to buy your house in the first place?"

"Not really. He just said he has always loved it." Joel banged the steering wheel with the heel of his hand. "He's a

93

jerk. It's probably to feel like he was winning against me at something."

He shook his head, as if he couldn't believe it. "He would always change the game. If I won once, he'd make it best of three."

CHAPTER FIFTEEN

*T*hey parked the car out the front, and Joel unlatched the gate. Bonnie came trotting around from the back yard of Hazel's place and followed them around past the tumbledown garage, sniffing at the shadows.

When they got inside, Bonnie walked up and stood close to Hazel, ready for an ear rub. Hazel threaded the soft ear between her fingers.

"I could rustle up some pizza if you want," Joel said.

"That sounds great." Hazel sat at the table, staring out at the garden.

Bonnie slumped down outside the door. *There better be some for me.*

She watched him pull a base out of the freezer and spread it with a tomato sauce, then sprinkle basil, and dot salami and mozzarella on top. The herby smell made her mouth water.

"We've got about half an hour," he said.

Joel came up behind her and entwined his warm fingers in hers. He dragged his other hand across her collarbone, raising goosebumps. She twisted to face him.

"I have to show you something." He led her to the ladder.

"Is this some sort—"

"Just look." At the top was a mezzanine floor with just enough space to stand. Before he turned off the light, she saw t-shirts on the floor and messy covers on the bed.

In the sudden darkness, she looked up. A thousand shining stars opened above her. It was a huge skylight. As she stared, more seemed to appear in the spaces between until it was a brilliant, twinkling mosaic.

"You look at this every night?" she said.

"I built it just for this view." He pointed up. "They all look the same at first but each one is completely different." And when she twisted around to kiss him, she thought she knew him a little more.

All of a sudden, the hairs on her arms raised up and she shivered. Bonnie's yelp split through her mind. Bonnie was in trouble, in a lot of pain. *Where are you,* she sent. *Where are you?*

Hazel jumped up, threw on her clothes and climbed down the ladder. She went outside, hardly noticing the cold grass underneath her feet. The air had that fresh smell like rain was coming.

Hazel walked fast, heart pumping, straight across the lawn, past the bushes, and down through the orchard, to the far end of the section. She shivered. A thin silver moon outlined the trees and the dinghy seemed to float ghostly in the dark.

Then she noticed the greyish-white of the tail. Bonnie was lying beneath the trees. Hazel ran over there, hardly daring to breathe, and bent down next to her.

Bonnie lifted her nose to Hazel's forehead. *It's just a broken leg.*

A woman stepped forward out of the shade.

"What the hell are you doing here?" Hazel cried.

"I own this place. And you?" Kirsten was immaculately dressed, in a navy dress and silver boots. Not a hair out of place in her blond bob.

Hazel stared at Kirsten, remembering her name from the company listing. But this woman worked with Christo. Why was she here at Joel's house? It didn't seem to make any sense.

"You own this?" Hazel asked. She knew it sounded stupid, but her mind seemed to be moving slower than reality.

"Good thing I do, too." She stepped forward and moved past Hazel, who caught her wrist.

"I thought Scott Hills bought this property?"

"That puppet?" Kirsten asked. "He is just my dogsbody." She stared at Hazel and twisted her arm, but Hazel only gripped on tighter.

"Will someone tell me what is going on?" Joel had followed her out here and was standing there with a hoodie and his Batman shorts on, with little bats dancing absurdly on the golden fabric.

Cool, fine rain was falling on Hazel now, making it hard to hold on to Kirsten's arm.

"This property is home to one of the most ancient species of magical creatures in the world. I had to buy it to look after its environment. I can't trust anyone else to look after it."

"*You* bought my place," Joel said. "Wait – did you say magical creature?"

Kirsten grimaced. "It was actually pretty easy. Hills told me where you work, Joel, so I made a dummy account and placed one bad review on one site 6 months ago. Worked like a charm."

"But... he loaned me some money," Joel said, numbly. He curled and uncurled his fists as if unsure who or what the enemy was.

Kirsten sighed. "Just for looks. He is very susceptible to suggestion, shall we say. When people think they are doing the right thing, it's all so easy. You can get them to do pretty much anything. It's all about the stories they tell themselves."

Hazel was shaking. "Joel, can you please carry Bonnie up to the house and call the Mornington vets? It's a broken leg."

"You're a witch," Hazel said when Joel had disappeared up the hill, carrying Bonnie in his arms.

"Now, Hazel. Let go of me," Kirsten said.

I am.

"So, you cursed my aunt?"

She pressed her lips together. *It was only a little curse,* Kirsten thought. *Until we could figure out how to get around her protections.*

Hazel remembered something, a blonde bob amongst the sea of faces in the crowd. "It was you at the speech. What were you trying to get Joel to drink?"

Kirsten sighed, but Hazel could feel her pulse racing in her wrist. "Nothing." *I added a little something to your water.*

"*My* water?"

I knew you would never keep out of it. So, I just thought a little memory potion might help. Look, it has all got out of hand, Kirsten thought. *All I wanted to do was save the last breeding colony of these lizards on the mainland. They are sacred guardians of knowledge.*

Kirsten's voice suddenly got louder, as if she was speaking

inside Hazel's mind. Hazel cringed as the sound reverberated inside her skull.

Let me go.

Hazel did her best to block it, gritting her teeth and closing her eyes, grabbing on to the wrist with both of her hands. To distract herself and Kirsten, she kept talking.

"How did you manage to fast-track the sale of the house?"

"What are these accusations?" Kirsten muttered, struggling to get away.

Mandy is my sister-in-law. She owes me for something she did to me a few years ago, so she was happy to help. It is amazing how having friends in the right places can make anything happen.

"You say you are trying to save these creatures. But you work for a developer?"

You have...

Kirsten twisted her wrist up and then down fast. It came free of Hazel's grasp.

... a backache. You will let me go now. I will leave the property, and you will not follow.

Hazel doubled over as pain shot up her spine. Kirsten walked off quickly.

The next morning, her aunt Briar turned up with Fritha and Moira. The pain in Hazel's back had gone as quickly as it came, and she was feeling confused but safe for the time being.

Her aunt still looked pale, but she was walking alright, and smiled widely at Hazel when she came inside. Hazel hugged her tight. *You're glowing*, her aunt thought.

"I'm so happy you are feeling better," Hazel said.

"Thanks to you, love. And what about you? Where's Bonnie?"

"At the vet," Hazel said, opening up the curtains in the lounge, and squinting in the light. "She'll be fine. I'm sure she'll be really happy if she has to have the Cone of Shame, though."

"I feel sorry for you having to deal with her attitude if that happens," her aunt said.

"Do you all want tea?" Fritha brewed up a hot restorative that smelled of chamomile and peppermint, and Hazel lit some candles. They sat down in the lounge, and Bonnie nestled her head under Hazel's arm, while she recounted the story.

"So, she cursed you to get you out of the way, Briar. In case you objected to the sale."

"I know of her, I think," Briar said. "She's a Treleaven from Andersons Bay. She offered to buy this place many years ago. So, I put a protective charm around it. And silly me, thought that was that. I didn't realize she was a witch."

"If only I'd been awake!" Briar frowned and one of the candles flickered out. "I could have helped."

"That's just it. Kirsten wanted you out of the way. But she also was desperate to have a meeting with you," Hazel said. She shook her head. "It's all very strange. Anyway, she said it's one of the only breeding colonies of this lizard left. *All of that* for environmental reasons." She waved her hand, encompassing the house sale, the attack on her aunt and the strange twilight meeting in Joel's garden.

"Hmm, I think there's a bit more to it than that. Where, did she say?"

They walked outside, down the steps.

"I see you've been keeping up the garden," Briar said. The vines on the verandah had new shoots of vibrant green. She reached out quickly, to hook into the vibrations of all the living things and felt the plants' energy.

Hazel wondered if they were growing again because her powers were back.

It can sometimes be a sign of new love, her aunt thought. Last night with Kirsten, Hazel knew she had learnt a lot more than she wanted to give. But Briar was a powerful empath and had a lot of skill at shielding her thoughts. If Hazel was hearing what Briar thought today, it was because she damn well wanted her to.

Hazel jumped up on the fence and pointed at the little well over on Joel's property. "Apparently, they live underground in this spring. I talked to Grannie Em about it."

Briar climbed up to have a look, then she put her hands on her hips, staring at the tree. "It's right next to the fence," she said. "We might have something here. I always knew us Redfernes had the luck of the ancients."

"What are you talking about?" Moira asked.

Briar's eyes were shining, and she walked up to the tree, inspecting its leaves. "This tree has the most amazing blooms, bright white with no space to spare, and I always suspected it was some sort of magical tree. But it must be because of the spring running beneath *both* our properties," she said.

"Now, don't get yourself too excited—"

"Moira, remember when we lived here and the Andertons first built that fence? We never got the boundary checked. I have a feeling we just told them to go for it."

"We did. We were a little preoccupied back then." Moira smiled at Briar.

"Hazel, we may have most of the spring, or even the whole thing, under our protection. Despite what Kirsten says," Briar said. "I don't even think she would realize that."

"One of the creatures died, though. Bonnie found it. Maybe we do need Kirsten to protect them," Hazel said.

Briar sighed. "That's a problem for another day. Today, I'm glad my toes are *above* ground."

As they walked back up to the cottage, her aunt sent her a little warning.

Tread carefully, though. I meant it before, you are shining like a beacon.

I am?

Find a way to close off your mind so you don't invade people's privacy. You are more powerful than you know. And others will notice, Briar said.

A little while later, Joel placed a teacup on her side table. He had insisted she lie down in bed and told her to wait there, while he went out to the kitchen.

"You've got a lot of herbs hanging up in there," he said, sitting down next to her.

Hazel nodded.

"You've also got a lot of candles."

"Yup," she said. "Is there anything you do like about me?"

"I really like how driven you are." He pressed his lips to her wrist and drew them slowly up her arm and tickled her bicep with his mouth. "You're so strong."

She squirmed. "I just keep swimming, that's all."

Hazel reached for her teacup. He waited for her to take a sip then folded her in his arms. His lips were soft and warm, but his eyes searched her face.

"Now tell me, how did you know where your dog was?" *I know you're keeping something from me.*

She put the cup down, and threaded her shirt through her fingers. "I knew she couldn't be too far away..."

"You walked straight there. Like a zombie." He grinned.

She hugged him tight so that he couldn't run away. "Once I said I'd accept anything about you, so I hope you'd do the same."

"All I know is when I've spent the day with you, I want to see you again. It's what I feel when I carve things, like the true beauty of it is hidden, and if I can only bring it out, it will be amazing. I want to work on this and see where it goes."

Tears pricked her eyes. She had never had to confess this to anyone, and she knew how it sounded. Insane. She wondered if he'd jump away from her like she was crazy.

Anyone who's had a good cup of tea when they really need it must believe in magic, Hazel thought. *Somebody who has stood on the crumbling ruins of a castle and felt the hair on the back of their neck lift. Somebody who stares into the heavens, searching for something more than dust...*

"I'm... different," she said. "My family are witches."

He laughed. "Like broomsticks and stuff?"

"Not exactly. I can sense people's thoughts."

"Haha," he said, as if waiting for the punchline.

She shook her head. "Not a joke."

He pulled away a little. "You're *not* joking, are you? Because you don't lie," he said. "I knew there was something about you. It all makes sense. You're so tightly wound all the time." She watched the wave of emotions flicker over his face; confusion to shock to realization. "You can control people's minds?"

She shook her head. "It's more like a radio broadcast but you give me a lot more information than you think you do."

In the silence, a tapping started upstairs. *Oh, Goddess,* Hazel thought.

"My thoughts are probably pretty predictable, are they?" *I want to kiss you all the time.*

She leaned forward and placed a kiss on his rough cheek.

Joel stared out the window, where a grey tabby cat was staring at them from the fence, its tail flicking back and forth. He put his hand next to hers and reached out his little finger. It was a gesture that said, *I'm here. I haven't run away yet.*

"So, what do we do now?" he asked.

"I've got a bathroom that needs some sidings," Hazel said. "And maybe a new door for the hot water cupboard. Look at this place, there's heaps to fix. I think you'd do a great job. And my aunt said she will pay half."

"You're staying at this house then?" Joel asked. "Are you going to stop looking for a house to buy?"

Hazel saw a frilly nightgown and some shiny silver hair appear through the ceiling light, then her Grannie's face appeared.

She pointed towards the roof. "I can't exactly leave *her* here, can I?"

The End

A NOTE FROM K M JACKWAYS

Hello! I hope you enjoyed Brand of Magic. You can find more of Hazel, Joel and the rest of the cast in Book 2 of the Redferne Witches - coming early 2021!

If you liked Brand of Magic, please consider reviewing it on Amazon or Goodreads. Every review helps!

Want more witchy fiction? Keep reading for an excerpt from Witching with Dolphins, and a list of all the Witchy Fiction books written by my friends and I here in New Zealand. If you'd like to find out more about us and our books, check out our website at https://www.witchyfiction.com or follow our Facebook page https://www.facebook.com/witchyfiction .

ABOUT THE AUTHOR

K M Jackways is a freelance writer and mother of two based in Canterbury. She loves shady green places and teaching animals to talk. Her fiction has been published in various magazines and anthologies, including The Best Small Fictions 2019. She has lived in random places, from Dunedin, New Zealand, to Bordeaux in France. Her stories expose the hidden lives of the past and the future, inspired by her background in psychology and linguistics.

EXCERPT FROM WITCHING WITH DOLPHINS BY JANNA RUTH

Despite having lived in Akaroa for her entire life, Harper never got tired of watching the sea come in, welcoming the magic it brought her. It was barely a tingle, but it filled her with a sense of peace and belonging that was hard to come by anywhere else. On a sunny day, Akaroa Harbour is full of magic. The water glistens in the sun like an endless tapestry of light. Waves crash against the harbour walls, rippling through the picturesque town set on the shore. Lush green hills roll into the sea, like the lava flows they're made of, once did. Dozens of white sails dot the ocean in between, and on the far end of the harbour, where the bay meets the Pacific, dolphins swim.

The Hector's dolphins roaming along the New Zealand shores are one of the smallest of their species. They're darker than their more famous cousins with a rounded back fin that is unique to them. Several groups frequent the bays of Banks Peninsula, drawing droves of tourists into the area. They come for the dolphins and stay for the beautiful French-heritage town hidden away in the harbour.

Harper owed today's trip to the seaside to her line of

work, yet she didn't exactly complain. Working for the Akaroa Mail, Harper was meant to take pictures of Ethan Hillborough, as he swam in the water with his dolphin. Of course, the dolphin was as much his as Ethan was hers. Being a witch herself, she knew all about his familiar, but to the rest of Akaroa, he was the dolphin whisperer; the guy you wanted on your 'Swimming with Dolphins' cruise because he always attracted at least one dolphin.

The dolphin's name was Ika, a silly name Ethan had given her when he'd been nothing more than a wool-headed teenager, and Ika no more than a motherless calf. Dolphins were not fish, but the name stuck.

Ethan had grown up considerably from the lanky youth he'd once been. His frame had filled out quite beautifully, Harper noted – not for the first time – through the lens of her camera. The muscles of his sun-kissed back contracted and relaxed with each stroke as he swam with Ika, trying his hardest to keep pace with her. Despite Ethan using his magic to propel himself through the water, the dolphin merely toyed with him.

Harper was still taking pictures, when Ethan pulled himself up on the pier and shook out his dark locks like a wet dog, spraying water everywhere. Running a hand through his hair to get it out of his face, he looked at her with a smile that could melt all the chocolate of "La Petite Sorcière", the little coffee-shop Harper called her home.

"Got enough pics?" he asked, a grin splitting his tawny face.

"Barely." Tentatively, Harper put the camera away and took out her notebook instead. "How's the water?"

Next to them, Ika was showing off her well-rounded dorsal fin as she slowly slid through the water.

"Not bad for late September. Could be a bit warmer, I guess, but Ika loves it."

A series of chattering noises rose in the air as the dolphin confirmed his words. Ethan's attention went straight to her. "Yeah, I know, lots of fish this time of the year." He shook his head. "Lazy dolphin."

If dolphins could glare, Ika would be doing just that.

Giggling, Harper took a seat next to Ethan, avoiding the wet patches around him. "Do you want that in the article? 'Dolphin whisperer reports dolphins are getting lazy as the weather warms up'?"

"I wish they'd stop calling me that." Leaning back on his elbows, Ethan turned his face towards the sun, soaking up its meagre heat.

Harper stole a glance at him, noticing the chiselled cheekbones and the strong curve of his nose, telling of his faint French and Māori heritage. "It's too late now. And besides, you are whispering to dolphins."

"One dolphin, and it's more of a back-and-forth-bickering than any sort of whisper." He glared at Harper for teasing him, but it only lasted for a second. "So, what's this piece about? Not another origin story I hope."

Ethan had found Ika tangled in an abandoned fishing net, half-starved from the time spent trapped in there. It had taken a lot of magic on his part to nurse the dolphin calf back to life. No one outside of their coven knew about that though, so when Harper had to report on the origins of their unique friendship, she had to make up half of it.

"Not this time." She made sure her cell phone was set to recording. "I'll interview you about the conversation efforts around the peninsula, and you can tell me how the Hector's dolphins are doing."

Naturally, Ethan's warm brown eyes lit up. He could talk

111

about conservation for hours, another reason why he had become the poster boy for Akaroa's cruise companies. "Well then, where do you want to start?"

Her pen ready to go, Harper didn't need to ponder that for long. "Let's kick things off by telling me about the current state of our dolphins. Any changes from last year? Future prospects?"

As Ethan launched into a lengthy account about Ika and her friends, Harper jotted down her notes.

"To be honest, Ika's worrying me," Ethan told Harper as they strolled through the streets of the former French settlement.

Instantly, Harper worried as well. Ika wasn't her familiar, but the dolphin was as dear to her as she was to Ethan. "Why?"

He shrugged. "I don't know. She's slower. I said lazy, but that doesn't really cut it." Sighing, he came to a stop. Their destination wasn't far now, but it became clear that he didn't want anyone else to know. "What if she's sick?"

Harper's heart went out to him. The trouble with binding yourself to an animal was their short lifespan. No one knew that better than her. She had bonded with a little blue penguin, called Leebee, when she'd been only eight. He had died before she'd come of age. His death had devastated her. It still hurt now when she thought about Ika and Ethan meeting the same fate.

"She's not old."

"She's not exactly young either," Ethan protested. Ika had been his familiar for almost fifteen years.

"What does she say?" Leebee hadn't been able to hide his pain and worries from her.

Ethan shrugged again. "Nothing. She's getting cagey when

I ask, so there's definitely something up. Bloody dolphin," he mumbled.

Harper reached out and stroked his arm. "I'm sure she's alright. It sounds like it's something she needs to work out for herself. Give her some space."

Snorting, Ethan shook his head. "Giving space isn't exactly what familiars do."

Want to read more? Click here to get Witching with Dolphins now!

MORE WITCHY FICTION BOOKS

Need more witchy goodness in your life? Check out the full list of Witchy Fiction books below!

Succulents and Spells (Windflower One), by Andi C. Buchanan: Laurel Windflower is a witch from a family of magic workers - but her own life is going nowhere until Marigold Nightfield knocks on her door. Marigold is a scientist from a family of witches, and she's in search of monsters. What lies ahead could reveal all Laurel's shortcomings to the woman she's trying to impress... or uncover the true nature of her power.

Hexes & Vexes, by Nova Blake: Small towns are full of gossip, and Mia is pretty sure that no one in her hometown of Okato has ever stopped talking about her. Cast off by her best friend, blamed for a local tragedy – Mia had no choice but to run away.

Now, ten years later, she's being dragged back.

Holloway Witches, by Isa Pearl Ritchie: Ursula escapes to Holloway Road leaving her former life in tatters following a bad break-up. She's looking forward to a quiet respite in a cozy cottage with a lush garden and lots of bookshelves, but instead she can't shake the eerie feeling she's being followed...

Overdues and Occultism, by Jamie Sands: That Basil is a librarian comes as no surprise to his Mt Eden community. That he's a witch? Yeah. That might raise more than a few eyebrows. When Sebastian, a paranormal investigator filming a web series starts snooping around Basil's library, he stirs up more than just Basil's heart.

Familiars and Foes, by Helen Vivienne Fletcher: Adeline yearns for family, but for years, the closest she's gotten is her assistance dog, Coco. When a frightening encounter with a ghost brings an old friend back into her life, it seems like Adeline's about to find the companionship she's been missing. But her crush might have to wait. As the ghost's smoky presence increases, Adeline feels its hold on those around her tightening dangerously.

Brand of Magic (Redferne Witches, Book One), by K M Jackways: Hazel Redferne is an empath witch but she's given up on magic. When her neighbour, Joel, needs her marketing expertise, Hazel jumps right in to help. But an attack on her powerful aunt means unlocking her psychic powers is the key to protecting the Redferne witches. Can Hazel let magic - and love - back in?

Witching with Dolphins, by Janna Ruth: Friends before magic (or boys) has always been Harper's prerogative. Her best friend Valerie is everything she is not: beautiful, confident, and the most powerful witch on Banks Peninsula. They might not see eye to eye on everything, yet, when a sinister scientist threatens their coven, Harper is willing to give up everything: the man they both love, her life, or even the little magic she has.

Made in the USA
Middletown, DE
28 October 2020